The Hunter

John Gamester

BALBOA.PRESS

A DIVISION OF HAY HOUSE

Balboa Press books may be ordered through booksellers or by contacting:

Balboa Press
A Division of Hay House
1663 Liberty Drive
Bloomington, IN 47403
www.balboapress.com
844-682-1282

Print information available on the last page.

ISBN: 979-8-7652-4098-4 (sc)
ISBN: 979-8-7652-4097-7 (e)

Balboa Press rev. date: 04/06/2023

Contents

Chapter 1   Carlos 1
Chapter 2   Tina... 11
Chapter 3   Carlos 24
Chapter 4   Ingrid 37
Chapter 5   Armand 46
Chapter 6   Jack.. 56
Chapter 7   Carol 64
Chapter 8   Jack.. 75
Chapter 9   Sal 82
Chapter 10   Jeff... 95
Chapter 11   Lily.. 103
Chapter 12   Tabitha 111
Chapter 13   Abby... 122
Chapter 14   Jasper 130
Chapter 15   Anna... 142
Chapter 16   Abby... 148
Chapter 17   Marie 157
Chapter 18   Carol 163
Chapter 19   Abby... 172
Chapter 20   Jack.. 177
Chapter 21   Gary 185
Chapter 22   Beth... 192

Chapter 23 The Thin Man 198
Chapter 24 The Trio... 205
Chapter 25 Jack.. 210
Chapter 26 Tristen 216
Chapter 27 Carol 224

Chapter 1
Carlos

THE SOUND OF THE ENGINE REVERBERATES OFF HARD concrete walls. A squeal of tires echoes from black tires as little red Porsche whips around the corner. Dashboard lights glare back at the shadowing pale driver as heavy concrete looms closer. Tires slow, then stop. Darkness returns as headlights flicker off. Silence. The door swings silently open. A tap from his leather loafer on the oil-streaked concrete pad. This ghostly driver steps into a dimly lit parking garage. His manicured nails pushing the door closed. He takes a deep breath, letting cool summer air fill his undead lungs. He grins as a faint smell of the sea reminds him of a time not so long ago when he was new at this game.

Well, not so long ago, his mind reminds him as his lips smirk.

A hum of dew on electrical wires brings an eyebrow up with confident arrogance. It's going to be a good night. His reflection in the mirror shows a pale face contrasted by the blackness of his tailored dress shirt and blood-red tie. The white of his tailored coat is closer to his complexion than the accent he keeps from his youth.

But the ladies do love a Latin lover. His smile dimples at the corners of his cheeks. Glistening fangs poke ever so slightly from the red lips that normally hide them. Porcelain hands clash with his red tie as he straightens the knot into its proper position.

There is a slight echo as the vampire's loafers break through the hum of power lines that disrupt the view of the cityscape beyond. Between the concrete barriers, lights of the city glows back at the vampire. His eyes shine slightly in the gloom of a fluorescent glow that comes from above.

I like this place, his thoughts drifting as the tapping of his loafers takes him closer to the filthy stairwell.

Tires squeal. Ripping through his pleasant thoughts. His mouth twists at the corners, revealing enlarged canines. Eyes follow a seventies-style van as it slips into a parking spot. A concrete barrier supports him as he glares at the beat-up junker, parked three spaces from his baby.

At least the asshole didn't park next to me. The last thing I need is a dent from some asshole redneck. His fangs disappear behind the calming expression. He shrugs, turns. A heavy metal door squeals as he steps into the stairwell.

Urine and vomit assault him.

I hate the stink of humans. His face twists in disgust. His loafers echoes off the painted, chipped, rust stained steel steps. He stops. His face twists.

That van. Have I seen it before? The vampire's ears perk

up. Silence greets his supernatural ears. A strand of hair slips out of its slicked-back place as the vampire shakes his head.

I'm being paranoid. That red-neck bastard is probably going to one of those titty bars that's closer to the poor part of town. Fuck him. His muscles flex under his coat. He feels the strength of his colossal frame. An arrogant smile flashed across his face.

Let the bastard try something. I'll just have to feed on something not so pretty tonight is all. The grin widens as the squeak of the fire door brings him back to the fresh air of the street.

The vampire stops, his ears pulling in all the sounds that surround him. His pale hand stopping the movement of the door. A groan of metal hinges above. The slight ring of the steel step as a heavy boot treads.

Bet it's that van guy. Should I call it an easy night? No, I want something pretty. The door swings slowly as the vampire struts away from the man that does not know how close he came to death. He smiles, the power of what he is pulsing through him.

Part of today's paper flutters down the street. A photo of a young woman taking up half the page. A headline says a killer is stalking the city. More girls are missing. The vampire ignores it. He knows the killer. He strolls toward the brightness of the Gas Lamp District. A rat scurries into a hole carved into the side of a Mexican restaurant, its shuttered windows dripping with rust. A cat struts on the other side of the street. The vampire shows some teeth. The feline returns the gruesome smile with a hiss. Darkness encompasses the cat as it slinks away.

This is what I like about this city. The quiet spots. Something I never had as a boy. No, Mexico City was so packed with human refuse I was lucky to have a moment to myself. The vampire thinks as he moves closer toward a trio of youths. Slacking pants, plated gold chains, silver and black sports themed jackets.

Yes, thugs.

He lets the sight of the young men leaning menacingly against the shuttered insurance business sink in. A glance, eyes scan the white suit. Whiteness at the corner of a thug's mouth, a gold tooth, breaks the ivory monotony. Stares at the two of them.

This IS like home. He grins. He can smell them, even as the scent drifts on a breeze that blows at his back.

No fear. His grin grows to a toothy smile. A yawn, fangs warn. A paleness washes over the boys, their heads bow. His toothy smile glaring at them as he passes. Sneakers pound the concrete, first loud, slowly drifting into silence.

Cowards. He thinks to himself as the lights continue to grow brighter. *But that is the way of the thug, isn't it? I should know. It was how I got my start. Running drugs. Extortion. Then he found me. The one that made me a god. Something so much more than human. Something that has power.* His grin grows as his chest swells. Pride in what he is courses through his undead heart.

The vampire turns the corner of a brick facade building. Light splashes out from the Gas Lamp District, illuminating his pale skin. His eyes take in the crowd that stands before him. His smile touches the edges of his mouth, lips sealed, concealing the enlarged canines within. Air sinks into his chest.

Now to find blood. His eyes dart across the signs as he glides through the crowd, old and young, mixing on the packed sidewalk. *Where to hunt?* His mind asks itself as the blue neon grabs his wandering eye. *Yes, the Enviro.* His laugh is for himself, kept inside, hidden from the masses that crush past one another in the brightly lit downtown party district.

Enviro, how do they come up with these names? Silly really. He thinks to himself as he moves closer to his hunting ground. His eyes drift across the line of youth that pushes past the little balconies the restaurants use.

Something youthful sounds tasty tonight. The Enviro it is.

Then a smell. Something dangerous. Oil, herbs, flowers. The kind a vampire fears. He stops. Sweat beads on his forehead. Not enough for a human to notice, but another vampire would see the fear forming in him. His eyes dart. Leaning on the corner of the building, he just rounded. A man.

I should know him. The vampire's forehead wrinkles. His eyes bore into the white tee with the four uneven black stripes. Ruffled short blonde hair. The vampire's eyes drift over the man. His faded jeans. Work boots. The bright blue eyes.

I know him. But from…

A crone shoulders past the vampire. His attention slips from the man to her ancient form. Her glare telling the vampire all he needs to know. Eyes back to the corner. He is gone. A sigh escapes the vampire's dry lips.

Must be nothing. You're getting paranoid, Carlos. You need to relax.

The vampire pivots. Strolls through the crowd. Head returning to the corner. Fear narrows his eyes. He knows that man. Something about him. Something to be afraid of. But he can't place it. Anger grows inside him as the thought of fearing a mortal crosses his mind.

"It's nothing." The fear and anger in his voice betraying the words he whispers to himself. Breath relieves some of the tension in the vampire's chest, then he turns. Eyes focus on the line. Youth in their revealing clothing. So joyful to get inside. Fingers retrieve a supple leather wallet from the white jacket pocket beside his heart. A crisp hundred-dollar bill slides past the others, into manicured fingers.

A monster of a man stands before him. His black beard branching out to his belly. Grease-laden hair pulled into a tight ponytail. His black jacket and pants blending into a black tee. A deep, jagged scar runs the length of his tanned Caucasian face. His scowl greets the vampire, shorter and in better shape than the hulk standing in front of him.

"Get to the back of the line." The hundred slips into the bouncer's hand. A quick glance. Slight grin. A nod from the oversized head and the vampire saunters past college kids that are complaining. The vampire glances back as the bouncer growls at the crowd. A toothy grin glimmers across the vampire's lips, then it disappears.

Light flickers from the dance floor beyond a beaded curtain. Behind a hole in the black wall, a pretty blonde waits for the vampire's money. The twenty disappears into a cash box under the table. Disgust greets his gaze.

This one does not like me much. A nod and he moves away with the glowing stamp placed firmly on his left hand. He looks at it, a unicorn reared up, ready to charge. The shake of his head is too slight for any human to notice, but it is there, for the unicorn.

He moves past the beads, into the flashing lights, another bouncer checks for the unicorn then nods for him to enter. The pounding of the beat touches his body, moving through it. The sound of pop music annoys him, it has the grating of a rusty fence to his sensitive ears. A grimace that is hidden by flashes of light and darkness creeps across his face. The wooden dance floor sits in the center of the room, full of college kids, its polish scuffed from numerous feet. He scans the room. High tops surround the dancers and beyond that, in the gloom, sits the standard tables and chairs. Black walls enclose the room.

The vampire is pushed slightly by a coed, her red hair and plump form reminding him of his youth. His eyes follow her to a high top. She slips onto her seat, the four other women ignore her. His eyes drift over the others. A pair of blondes. Thin, pretty. Their focus on two men dancing. He can see the flush of desire redden their cheeks. Eyes move to the other pair. A girl cries, her friend's arm around her, compassionately. The redhead looks out at the dance floor, her eyes dulled with boredom. The vampire shifts through the crowd, moving closer to the girl.

This is the one for tonight. He tells himself, focusing on the girl. *She's the outsider. The one that won't be missed. Not until it's too late. Now to get close enough to get into her head. To control her. Then, make her bend to my will.*

The vampire slips past the ones he has no interest in. Darkness hides his pale skin, slightly visible fangs that are just peeking behind the red lips. His grin, evil if those in the club could only see, disappears as he slips a hundred dollar bill into the waiting hand of the bottle service girl. Her bright red lipstick grins with greed at his pale form, though the white suit helps to hide the lack of tan the vampire's skin has.

Carlos' eyes remain on the girl, her red hair enticing him, as the short pleaded skirt of the bottle service girl bounces in the air, revealing a pair of little red panties. Her head turns to grin at what she thinks is a man, as the vampire slips into a plush chair. The wood table, polished to a fine sheen, reflects disco light up at the vampire, giving him some color.

He leans back, letting the music move to the back of his mind. A mind that begins to focus on the red head seated with a group of women that pay her no mind. His grin returns, then disappears as the cheap champagne at an overpriced cost is placed on the table in front of him. The short skirt, facing the vampire with the desire of a larger tip, exposes her red panties once more. A better view this time, the thin fabric giving a hint of what is hidden beneath.

The bottle service girl straightens, grins and winks.

"Anything else, sir?" The sound of her voice is deeper that the vampire would have expected, but it is no matter to him. This little barmaid with the revealing clothes. He wants an early night, not one that sees the club closing around him.

"No, I think that that will be all." The smooth Latin accent brings a quiver to the bottle girl's lip. Slight. Only his supernatural eyes catch it. He nods and the girl trips as she moves away from Carlos, seeking another rich customer that is willing to part with their money for the privilege of not sitting with the rest of the crowd.

The girl looks around the room, her red hair caressing her back. The vampire grins, it's the hair is what is making him desire her and he knows it. The plump form, enticing as it is, is only secondary. Those crimson locks remind him of something that he hasn't know in fifty years. Something he misses. Something that is gone forever. He watches the girl, focuses his mind once again. Reaching out, touching the girl's inner thoughts with his own. Letting the connection solidify. Letting the link between them grow.

The suggestions are soft. The desire to use the restroom. To leave this place. To leave the women she is with. The disgust in the redhead's eyes makes it clear that there is little suggestion needed. The crying girl is moving to hysterics. The friend beside her talking and angry that the others are not interested in the horrid break up that the cryer has just experienced. The blonde girls. Eyes on the two men on the dance floor. Moving with a seduction that has enamored the blondes. Carlos can see the clinching of thighs, the slight reddening of the cheeks. The amorous look in their eyes. And the role of the red head's.

Carlos can see the link forming between their minds, he and the red head. Can feel her mind fogging. As is so common when the suggestions begin to take effect. His grin is slight, exposing no teeth, as she looks around and finds his eyes on her. She looks away, slipping off the little high top stool. He can see the weakness in her legs, a good sign. His grin grows, a fang, to long to be human, is exposed. It disappears behind the pale pink lips as he watches the girl move away, toward the ladies room, toward the line of women waiting to get inside.

Chapter 2
Tina

TINA RAMBLES IN HER MIND. *WHAT THE HELL'S COMING over me? It's like somebody slipped something into my drink, but I haven't drank anything so that's not possible. Crap my head is fuzzy. Like I'm spinning.*

She shakes her head as she passes the line of under-dressed coeds. Pink neon from the ladies' room shines out at her like a beacon in the fog. Her legs wobble slightly, she feels her strength slipping away. Her hand grips a grimy door frame. Women in line glare at her as she steadies herself.

"Hey, skank. The line starts back there." A mini skirt, tube top wearing chunky girl sneers. Tina's shoulder twists as pink colored fingernails digs into her flesh. She stumbles, catches herself. Another girl, ugly and mean-looking blocks the angry one.

"Leave her alone, Lynn." The ugly girl's voice drifts to Tina's ears. It's distant. Dream-like. Her hand grips the pink door frame. Her legs failing to do their job. She's never been this close to the frame. She can see the peeling pink paint, black beneath. The grime is clear too.

Filth. Her mind screams as her hand shoots away. Her stomach retches. Disgust settles on her face.

Her head clears a little. Straightening, she steps into the crowded restroom. Two stalls. The sound of a flush. The smell of cheap perfume. Eyes glare judgement at her. She leans against the wall. Women move around her, anger peering at her. A coed, maybe twenty-one, steps beside her. She looks at Tina. A pause. Compassion. Then moves on. Tina wills her legs to strengthen, to get her to one of the two dirty sinks. She leans, arms helping the weakening legs. Her reflection shows no sign of anything. Except for a look of exhaustion. A deep breath clears some of the fog that muddles her mind. A shaky hand turns on the rust speckled tap, cold water splashes down the drain. She runs her hand under the water, letting the cold seep into her skin. Splash to her face. The cold wakens her. The fog dissipates slightly, but it is still there, she can feel it gnawing in the back of her mind.

"Are you ok?" A girl asks. Her silver bell voice brings a pleasant sensation to Tina. She looks at the girl. Blonde. Pretty. The ponytail doesn't help to age her.

She looks like she's in middle school. High school at the most.

"Yeah, something I ate." Tina's smile is weak, forced. The girl takes a paper towel. Wets it and places it on Tina's forehead. The wet soothes her. Brings her focus back, though not fully. Tina looks at the lithe girl, smiles, she feels stronger now.

"Thank you." The weakness in Tina's voice is leaving.

"You still look pretty pale." The high schooler's

youthful face twists with care. "Someone might have slipped you something. You might want to get out of here before you wake up in some seedy hotel, some fat asshole on top of you."

The shock of the words comes over Tina as she looks at the girl.

Fuck that's hard. The girl's eyes show wisdom that doesn't match her age. *This has happened to her.*

Tina's eyes widen. The realization sickens her. The girl's mouth contorts, her the childish face jerks away from Tina's. Then, those teenage eyes return to look into Tina's own. Tina watches girl's brow furrows. Become serious.

"Anyway, you better get out of here. Do you have a ride home?"

"Yeah. I can get home ok. Thank you."

The high schooler's smile lacks belief. A discomfort pulses through Tina's spine as the girl pushes her way past the rest of the women in the little restroom. Tina's gaze returns to the mirror. The flush is gone. She feels better, though the fog is still toying with her thoughts.

"It's time to go." A soft voice seeps out of her. A deep breath and she straightens. She turns to the door. Lynn glares at the entrance. Tina's middle finger greets the bitch's lear.

Tina sees her friends, they go double, then back to normal. Her legs buckle under her. She grasps for something, anything. Her fingers wrap around the back of a high-top chair. A weak smile greets the man with a cocked eye. His face is curious, though not interested.

"You ok?" The indifference in his words remind her

that she is alone. A feeling that she can't shake, almost overwhelming in its persistence.

"Fine, just too much to drink." She looks at the exit, cheeks reddening from the lie as the man returns his eyes to the dance floor and away from her. She can feel the strength returning to her legs, she straightens, smiles politely at the college guy who winks from the other side of the table, and takes a deep breath. She watches him shrug and return to the girl at the table beside him. Her disinterest apparent, even to Tina's fogged mind. She shakes her head, trying to clear it.

What the hell is going on with me? I have to get out of here. Get home. Get in bed. Maybe someone did slip me something. One of those girls. They're always telling me to lighten up, have some fun. Hard to have fun when you're the babysitter all the time. Haven't drank in public for months, now this is happening. Crap.

She slips through the hanging beads that separate her from the street. The heat of the club on her back, a breeze caresses her face. The smell of night. Refreshing, reinvigorating. She takes it in. Letting it fill her lungs. Hoping it will clear her mind.

The beads that separate the dance floor from the ticket booth create a prisoner's view. Mary's hand strokes the bared chest of one of the dancers. Her teeth glimmer in happiness. The boy, his drunken eyes marveling at her low cut top. The breasts pushed out for maximum effect. Shelly's mouth pressed hard against the other boys, eyes closed, nostrils wide. Her hand on his ass, his moving up her dress. Sara and Ann missing, no, they're at another table. Hate beams out of Sara's eyes. Ann's hands up in peacekeeper mode.

There's no way I'm getting involved in that. They can find their own way home. A sneer creeps across Tina's face, disgust at the women she has chosen to spend her night with. A hate that is so unlike her, but she can't help the loathing she feels.

I need air. I need to get out of her. Get away from those bitches and their bullshit.

Then she sees him. A man. Large, though not a giant. The workman's clothing so unlike what is common in this club. The strips on the white tee. Four black bars. Uneven. She knows it. Something her older brother was into. A band maybe. Her head won't let her focus. He is moving toward her. Calm. But the eyes are somewhere in the crowd. Not on her. He bumps a big college guy. A football type. Lineman maybe. Drinks fall. A tiny girl. Her white dress, the kind that barely covers her well formed body, is soaked in beer and red wine. She screams and the working man shrugs and tries to move past. The lineman grabs him. Swings. The rest of the footballer players move in. Tina feels bad for the working guy as she moves out of the club and into the street.

A blast of cool hits her as the night sky comes into view. A pimple-crusted boy's eyes drift up and down her body. Winced eyes great his leer and his face reddens. His friend laughs. She can feel his eyes on her ass as the click of her heels takes her away from him and his laughing friend. The exhaust from the street hits her hard, she stumbles, reaches out for anything. Nothing. She stumbles slightly. A firm grip meets her outstretched arm. The powerful limb steadies her, keeps her off the filth of the sidewalk. Passerby's look. Say nothing.

The city. The words roll in her head. She looks at him. Taking in the white suit. The skin that is almost as pale as the jacket. The black of the man's shirt contrasting. The red tie, giving a warning somewhere deep inside her.

"You look like you had a little too much to drink." A Latin accent, the kind you find in romance movies. It's pleasant, easy.

Trusting is the word you're looking for Tina. She tells herself as the red ties warning slowly recedes.

Her other hand touches the light linen, slides to the shoulder, her legs hold. She can feel a desire growing within her, she pushes it down. She looks up, a tight-lipped smile greets her. She steps back. Takes a breath, trying to control the emotions that she is repressing. The crowd moves around her. Around him. They take no notice of the pair standing on the sidewalk. A couple in the minds of the masses. This excites her, she doesn't understand why, but likes the feeling. He cocks his head, an eyebrow raises slightly. There is something sensual about it.

"Thank you." Her voice cracks, her face reddens. The embarrassment cuts to her core. "I'm not feeling well."

"I can tell." The grin widens but the lips remain firmly pursed together. "My sister sent me out here to check on you. She saw you in the restroom. Said she thinks someone slipped you something. A roofie I believe they are called." The words come easy and slow, thickened with a Mexican accent.

"Your sister?" Caution cuts through. The first real

fear of this man that she has felt. She eyes him, distrust building. Still the desire, longing, is still there. Eating at her.

"Yes. The blonde. Looks too young to be in here. That one. At the sink." His eyes stay focused on hers. He leans back, casual, against the cinder block wall.

"Oh." A whisper escapes her lips. The red cheeks of embarrassment return as the thought of this man causing her harm melts away. She looks at him, suave and confident. She smiles slightly, looking away as she does so. No longer sure of herself as the fog in her head grows thicker.

"She asked me to check on you when she saw you leave. Make sure you're ok. So, you ok?"

"No, but I can get a cab. I can get home without any trouble." A wobble in her knees brings the almost black eyes down to her legs. Those eyes move back up to meet her own. She feels as if those eyes touched her soul and a chill runs down her spine. A pleasant chill. He moves toward her. The pursed smile leading the way toward her. She struggles inside. Not sure of what to do. Her mind, it doesn't want to work. His words bring her back to the real world.

"I think not. I can get you home quicker than a cabbie. Anyway, my sister would never let me live it down if I didn't get you home safe." His shrug gives her the sense she doesn't' have a choice. Part of her likes this. Another, the one that sits deep inside grows angry at the thought of needing this man to take her home. "But if you really want a cab, I'll call one for you. There isn't any on the street." Her eyes pull from his. The traffic moves at a crawl. Sports cars, trucks, sedans, but no cabs. She knows he's right. A cab could be an hour on a night like this. The traffic of people shuffling from suburb lined streets to the party world of downtown. She looks at the black eyes, the pale lips and nods. Giving in to the idea of this man taking her home. She holds on to this power, trying to use it's strength to carry her forward.

"Alright. But just home." As the words leave her lips, she can feel her strength slipping away again. Anger boils up inside her, as her body leans against this strange man. She hates it, the weakness and fog that she feels. She looks at him beside her. His arm wrapping around her shoulders. Keeping her body from falling to the ground. Then a gratefulness comes over her. She realizes that her feelings are bouncing all around. Anger, fear, dependence, desire.

God, what is going on in my head. She screams to herself.

The pair move toward the dark edge of the Gaslamp district. Tina feels her feet slipping on the concrete, the strength of the man's arms holding her up, the glare in his eyes at the drunk coed that slams into Tina's shoulder. The giggles drift into the air as the crowd thins. Lights dim and grow less frequent. Buildings grow less pretty. Her eyes widen slightly as the fear of leaving the crowd sinks in. Her eyes dart as the filth of a part of downtown that she does everything to avoid after dark, and most times in the light of day, surrounds her. She looks up at him. There is no fear on the pale face. Eyes forward. Arms holding her close and safe against the wobble in her legs.

"Where are we going?" A tremble of a voice comes from the girl.

"My car's in that parking garage there." A pale finger juts out at the concrete structure.

His hand, it's so pale. So white. It has to be the light. Washing him out. Her eyes drift to her own hand, tanned and soft. His grip keeps her up. She looks at him, she can see his thoughts are not on her.

Maybe he's worried about his sister. But there's something about her. Something that's off. OH! She doesn't even look like him. Other than the paleness of their skin. Her white-blonde hair, his jet black. The accents, so different. Her, not American, foreign, something from Europe.

Her eyes move to the face, the one that seemed so charming not so long ago. She pushes away, looks at him. Distrust is in her eyes. His face twists into questioning.

"Your sister?" The words are venom.

"Yes?" His tone is soft as he looks at her. The same look as before, at the club.

"She, well, doesn't look much like you, does she?" A tremor of anger in the voice, with a touch of fear that seeps in behind.

"She's adopted." His close-lipped smile returns, the black eyes warm behind the almost white mask of a face.

"Oh." Relief washes over her. The fear dripping away. Embarrassment returns. The fog in her head thickens. She feels as if her mind is slipping away from her, that someone is taking it from her.

"My family came from Mexico when I was a boy. My father opened a taco shop. Worked hard. Long hours. We all did when we were old enough. Good trade to have. Making food." His tight smile beams down at her as his arm slips around her again, his strength leading her toward the garage that seems not so far away anymore.

"What's that have to do with your sister." Her voice slips into a whisper. Her will sipping away. She knows this and can do nothing to stop it. She hates the feeling.

"We did well for ourselves. The family that is. My father would see children living in filth. Hungry. He looked into what he could do. Taking kids in was what he found. So my parents used their newfound wealth to take in the children their adoptive country didn't want." Shoulders shrug. She eyes him, surprised. Shocked. An admiration brewing within her.

The scrap of metal on metal as the door opens onto the garage's stairwell. Fluorescent light hurts her eyes as they try to adjust from the darkness of the street. Her nose wrinkles as the smell of urine and vomit hit her nostrils. She stops a gag from going any further. She looks at him. Her eyes questioning this place. He smiles.

"It's cheap." The man shrugs, his uneasy smile raises one side of his lips. She follows him up the stairs, her shoes ringing on the metal steps giving a musical quality to the climb. She smiles, though the smell is horrid, the feeling of being looked after, of being helped is nice. She accepts it, letting it take her over. He turns to look at her, his black eyes kind and generous. She smiles, not sure what else to do. She is letting herself get carried away with this guy.

He's too nice. She thinks to herself. *He's the kind of guy that you would want to date. Maybe marry. Caring, kind, thinks of others. It's like an old-fashioned type in a young body. Like he's too good to be true.*

The door waits for her to go through, his hand stopping it from closing. He gestures for her to go first, gentlemanly, the close-lipped smile returning. Her smile is less certain. The ring of her heels changes from steel to concrete. His step quickens, he moves beside her, taking her hand in his. His smile, while still feeling something is not right about it, is friendly and kind. Like the rest of him. They stop at a red sports car.

Expensive. He has money. Or his parents do.

She pauses at the back of the car. Not sure what to do. The fog overcomes her thoughts. It's hard to think straight. Hard to think at all. Weakness in her legs, like before, only stronger. She hates this and tries to shake it off.

"Are you ready to go?" He turns to her. Her legs buckle. He moves quickly. Takes her in his arms, cradles her weakness in his strength. She looks up. A tear forms in the corner of her eye. Her voice is gone. She wants to scream at the fangs that bare down on her. The smile turning to a gap of death.

The smile, she tells herself. It was always the smile. Her head clears, but her muteness remains. I saw it. Those teeth. Why didn't I realize what it was?

The stink of rotten flesh that breathes out from behind those fangs. They move closer. She screams as loud as she can, but no sound escapes her lips. The pain of two daggers plunging into her neck. Blood is pulled from her veins. The pain is unbearable.

I can't move. I can't scream for help. I am dying and this thing is killing me.

She wills herself to live. She looks at the black hair

that brushes her cheek. The sensation so unlike anything she has felt. Pain mixed with pleasure. Numbness in her neck, pain in her veins. She can feel the consciousness leaving her. Her eyes widen, not from the pain, but from the realization.

It was this thing. It made me feel drunk, out of control. It was this monster that made me leave. I remember now. The voice in my head. Telling me to leave my friends, turning my thoughts against them. It was this pale-faced demon with its trusting eyes.

Her eyes flutter. Close. The vampire's fangs slip out of the lifeless body. His face flush with fresh blood. He straightens, the blood flowing through his veins.

Then pain boils through his chest.

"Fucking vampires." A deep raspy voice growls as the vampire's body crumples. Tina's paleness blending with the creatures. His eyes dart. *What has he done to me?* The vampire's voice is gone, only thoughts remain. Fear creeps into those eyes. Pain too. A heavy work boot, black and scuffed, crunches in front of those eyes.

"How's it feel to be the one that is helpless?" The growl is close. Anger is in those words. Hate.

The vampire struggles, but its body can't move. The large man towering over him, looking at the blood dribbling out of the corner of the vampire's mouth, staining the concrete. A faint grin. A human grin. The vampire's collar grows tight against his throat as his body lifts off the hard concrete.

"It's a stake, vampire." The creature's eye roll in its head. Unable to move, to threaten. Pain searing its chest.

"I can see you want to talk. That'll come later." The vampire's frozen face inches away from the blue eyes that burn with hate. "You'll tell me everything I want to know."

The vampire's eyes drift to the uneven black bars on the man's tee. They widen in recognition.

It's the bastard in the van. He followed me. Pain winces through the vampire's body. Glass, pebbles, bits of filth slide past the vampire. His body dragged to the van only a few spaces away.

A thud. The vampire looks at the grey of the concrete pad. Stained with the oil of who knows how many cars. The stink of a crushed cigarette sickens him. A click, he strains his eyes. The pop of a latch of a door handle, the faint squeak of the metal on metal. Not quite oiled enough. Grey concrete, then the stabbing pain of sudden movement. An electric shock of pain as the air swishes past, no it is he that is moving, not the air. Darkness, but his vampire's eyes tell him that the metal container is the back of the van. Another stink, garlic. Wild rose. Fear grows in him. Another click, a squeak. His limp body shifts under the rocking of the van. He is on his side, facing the man in the driver's seat. The bastard that did this to him.

"Wild roses and garlic, vampire. They'll keep you weak. That's if you didn't already know that. Funny how many of your kind don't know what is bad for you." The eyes bore into the vampire. The anger and hatred.

Did I kill someone he loves? The vampire doesn't know. *I've killed so many over the decades.* The rumble of the engine, a lunge, and the van is backing out.

The vampire watches, waiting for its chance. It doesn't come.

Chapter 3
Carlos

THE QUIET OF THE SLEEPY SUBURBAN STREET IS BROKEN BY the hum of the van. Eucalyptus trees hang into the car lined street. A lone walker, his dog in tow, sleepily shuffles down the cracked and uneven sidewalk. Headlights glare back into the driver's blue eyes as the van turns into a driveway. The click of the remote, the clunk of the garage door as it pulls itself up. An almost empty void lit by the van's eyes. Inside a heavy steel gun safe sits against the wall beside the door to the house's kitchen. Oil stains the concrete. Boxes line the outer wall. A single bulb fails to compete with the van's headlights. Work boot push the gas pedal and the van moves slowly into the man-made cave. Another click and the door trembles back down, concealing the van.

The vampire wills itself to move. Nothing happens. The man shifts. Looks at the stake. Wedged between the ribs, through the vampire's unbeating heart. The vampire's eyes wince. Hatred beams at the man. Inside the vampire screams. No sound is heard. The man smiles. The four black uneven bars on the shirt reminding the vampire of something it can't quite grasp. Of another time. The near black eyes of the vampire move up to look the in the man's blue eyes that peer back at the monster.

"We're home." The gravel in his deep voice shocks the vampire.

It looks at him with angry eyes. The door handle is pulled by heavy working hands. Calloused, tan. The metallic sound of the door opening drifts to the man's ears, as well as the vampires. Work boot steps onto the concrete. The door closes. A smell of garlic and wild rose is in the air. It sickens the vampire. Light blinds the creature as the back of the van opens to the garage. The man stands, his heavy hands reach in. The vampire screams inside, but no sound escapes it's lips. Those calloused hands drag the limp form toward it. It's staked paralyzed body slips off the edge of the van, slams onto the concrete with a silent scream of pain.

The man looks down. A sneer whips across his stubbled face. The point of the stake facing up at glaring eyes.

Contempt in those eyes. The thought drifts through the man's mind. *It hates me. Good. I can use that.*

Pain rips through the vampire's chest, the stake twisting as it's body is dragged toward the metal gun cabinet. The man's iron grip bruises the vampire's ankle. A tear drops silently from the corner of the creature's eye. The leg drops hard on the garage floor, as the man looks, the vampire's eyes face away from him. The creature is blind to him. He grins.

Good. The malice drips even in his thoughts.

Thick fingers flip the false electrical outlet. A keypad reveals. He looks down, the vampire is motionless, it's stake remaining fixed in his heart. 8-1-2-6-3. A hiss. The smell of garlic and rose. A pop. The side of the gun cabinet by the keypad swings slightly open. Blackness in the crack. Heavy hand pulls the door toward him, silently. Gloom hints at the edge of the strong wooden stairs. Stairs that are attached to the concrete walls, leading down into the blackness before the man and his vampire prey. He reaches in, flips a switch. Light springs into the stairway that leads to another door that is at the bottom. A metal door, rust dusting the bottom, waits for the man to open it.

He grasps the vampire, lifting it easily. Shifting it, dropping the creature's waist on his wide shoulder. The vampire's eyes read the brand of jeans the man is wearing. It sees little else. The sound of the cabinet closing softly behind them. Pain jolts the vampire with each step into the abyss. He stops, swings the door open, steps inside.

The perfume of garlic and rose is strong, stronger than the van. Stronger than the garage. The man takes the scent in. It soothes him. His eyes drift across the bootleg basement. The concrete floor. A drain in the middle of the room, the stainless steel of the table above the drain shimmering in the fluorescent light. The bare walls at the corner where the man stands, his prey slumped over his shoulder. The workbench across from him. Glittering means of torture that wait beg to be used. A steel shutter to his right. His boots echo slightly off the concrete. The vampire flips through the air, slamming onto the table, pain in the monster's eyes. Stake pushing further out of the chest. A silent scream from the motionless mouth. The man takes a thick leather strap, loops it around the vampire's leg. Cinches in tight. Moves around the potted wild rose at the corner of the table, binds the second leg. Moves along the garlic-lined edge to the arm, binding it, then the chest, then the last arm. The creature's forehead is lashed to the stainless steel table, between a pair of potted wild roses. The vampire glares out it's hate. Trying to use it's mind powers. Failing.

"Your mind tricks won't work on me. I can feel you trying to get a grasp on my will. The roses and garlic have made you too weak." The man's smile is not friendly. His thick fingers wrapped around the stake. The point looking up at him. Wickedness flirts across his lips. Rip. Blood splatters. The vampire screams. Pain distorts the creature's face. A hole in the vampire's chest shrinks until there is nothing there. Blood drips from the thick end of the stake, held in the man's muscular fingers. The drip slows. Stops. The blood dries, crusting the oak stake. The eyes of the vampire roll in pain, then settle on the man's grim face.

"I'll kill you for this. You do know that don't you. You bag of blood." The vampire's hiss brings a corner of the man's mouth up. A grim smile. A ring of the stake bouncing off the concrete. The vampire's body tries to jump, straps keeping the creature in place.

"No, no you won't." The tap of the heel of the man's boot rings softly as he steps close to the fanged lips. "I do have questions for you though. And you will answer them. Or, I will do things to you that you will never forget. Never recover from."

The man's face moves in closer to the vampires. The creature snarls, its head tries to lash out at the man. The leather strap holding it in place. He moves back, slowly, deliberately. His face is calm. There is that slight smile that the vampire is beginning to detest.

"I have friends. Friends that will hunt you down. Torture you. Make your death a living hell." Snarls come through bared fangs.

"I'm sure you do. Most of them know who I am. Or at least what I am." A hands light touch on the leather strap, the buckle inspected.

"And who the hell do you think you are?"

"I'm Jack the hunter." A wink at the vampire, its face turns from loathing to fear. Vampiric eyes dart across the room, hope leaves them.

"What? What do you want from me?" A tremor cracks the vampire's voice.

"I want to know where your maker is. That's it. Nothing more." Jack's hip shifts slightly, weight redistributing.

"I don't know what you're talking about."

"I think you do. I think you know where Tristen is. Yes, I know that he made you. That it happened in Mexico City. In the fifties. That you were a street rat, running through the shitty parts of the city. Picking pockets, hustling drugs. I know all about you. About the girl you loved. How she left you for a better man. A thug that was stronger, better connected. Had more money. I know about you helping a vampire, a vampire named Tristen when the sun was coming up. Hiding that monster in a shack, threatening to expose the sun on that fragile vampire skin if he didn't turn you into a vampire right then and there. The drink, the turning. Yes, I know about you, Carlos. And now I want to know where Tristen is." The monotone words flow smoothly from Jack's hard lips. The anger contained within him. Burning to get out.

"I swear. I don't know where he is. I haven't seen him in years." A tear slides down the side of the vampire's face, absorbed by his black hair.

"Is that so?"

"Yes, yes it is. Look. I don't know where Tristen is. I haven't seen him in decades. He left me. Said I was scum. Trash." Pleading turns to snarls.

This thing might be telling the truth. Jack eyes the vampire, as it struggles uselessly against the leather straps.

"You can't break free, vampire. Those straps are coated with garlic oil. You're stuck until I let you go. Now, what do you know about Tristen?" Arms across his chest, leaning against the table, looking down at the vampire's frightened eyes.

"Nothing. I hate him. He made me. Brought me here. To America. To this city. He made me a slave. Less than a slave. He's sick. Enjoys torturing others." The words fall out of the vampire's trembling lips. His eyes settling on the workbench, the tools of torture. "What are you going to do to me?"

"That depends on you. Depends on what you tell me. How useful you are. And don't give me that crap about Tristen being a monster. I know a monster when I see one and you're one of them. You lured that girl to her death. If I hadn't knocked that damn drink on the little bitch she'd be alive." The sneer frightens the vampire. It feels trapped, helpless.

"No, you don't understand." The accent thickening. "I have no choice. I have to feed. You can't imagine the pain if you don't." Pleading eyes follow Jack's tense body lift from the table. Garlands of garlic sway as the thud of work boots move across the basement.

"No, I don't think I can. But I do know pain. At least of a type. Your maker, your master, well that thing gave me pain. A pain that you can not imagine. No, vampire, I know pain. And soon you will too." Jack's fingers glide across the silver blade shining in the fluorescent light as it sits on the workbench. His caress brings a slight smile. "That monster took something from me that can never be replaced. Something more precious than anything you may try to bribe me with. So keep your promises of money, power, whatever. All I want from you is the location of Tristen. So, vampire, do you have what I want?" Jack's hand grips the dagger, the vampire's eyes widen. The creature trembles at the grim face, the tension showing as the body leans back on the oak bench.

"No. I swear. I told you I don't know. He could be anywhere. He could be here for all I know." Tears drip onto the steel table. The vampire's pitiful look does little to melt Jack's heart.

"Nice." Jack steps heavily on the concrete. Letting the creature that is bound to the table hear him move closer. "Begging will get you nothing. Tears? Is that some kind of trick to make me feel something? Make me think you are human? You can't fool me. I see through you."

The vampire's face hardens as Jack steps beside the table, dagger held lightly in his fingertip. The glare returns.

"Well. I tried the sob story. Now what hunter?" Carlos' tone is hard, emotionless. Dead.

"We find out where Tristen is. You are going to give me something useful or I am going to have a large pile of dust to clean up." The calm in Jack's voice touches a fear in Carlos that it hasn't felt in decades. It looks, trying to get inside the man's head. To read his thoughts, find out just what he is willing to do. The vampire knows that some of these hunters are mad. Some sadistic. Some, most, are full of shit. But not this one, he is different and the vampire can see that. And the stories. Nightmare tales of the demon that hunts his kind. One word. Jack.

"You're not getting in my head, vampire." Jack leans close, looking into Carlos' black, soulless eyes. The blade grazes the creature's hand. Carlos jumps, the bonds digging into his flesh. Jack straightens, takes the creature in with his eyes. Carlos glares, struggles. Fear grows in creature strapped to the table.

"Now, vampire, let's get serious about this little talk of ours." The blade glides across the silk shirt, stopping at the tie's red knot.

"Fuck you." Venom oozes from the pale lips that tremble slightly with the fear of what is to come.

"Not likely. Can your kind even do that?" The blade drifts to the creature's waist, his eyes following as best they can, Jack's eyes watching the vampire's.

"Even if you do cut me up it won't stick. You know that don't you? A hunter like you." The gloating eyes taunt Jack. His smile alarms the vampire.

"I do know that a steel blade will hurt. But a silver one. Like the one I have at your gut, well, that will do permanent damage." The vampire's eyes widen. True fear grips it. A thin sweat forms on its brow. Pleading eyes look at Jack's hard ones.

"No." A near breathless sound escapes Carlos' pale lips.

"Yes." The blade settles at the vampire's pinky. Carlos' eyes struggle to see what it feels.

"You can't. I'll be deformed."

The scream deafens Jack. The vampire's twisted expression. The finger, sliced, turns to a fine gray powder, not unlike the color of the concrete that some of the dust falls onto. Jack steps back. The joint, where the pinky once was, has healed.

So quickly. Amazed on the inside, Jack remains expressionless before the vampire's tearing eyes. *Now, this thing knows that it's in trouble. Now I might get some real answers.*

"Where. Is. Tristen?" More a growl than a question hisses from Jack's tight lips, his teeth baring as if he was the thing he despises the most in the world.

"I don't know." Jack can hear the defeat. He can hear the truth of the words and despises them all the same. His hand moves the ring finger. The vampire's eyes widen. Scream. Dust.

Jack lets the vampire calm himself. Two fingers missing. Disfigured. The vampire, pain distorting his youthful face, begs with his eyes. Jack can see that all hope is gone. That there is nothing to get out of this thing laying strapped to a table.

"Where?" The blade moves to the middle finger. The vampire looks away, a light sob drifts to Jack's ears.

"I don't know. Go ahead. Cut it off. I'll still not know. You can mark me up. Turn me into a nightmare vision. I still won't know. I can't tell you something that I don't know." The words come softly, slowly, without hope. Jack knows they are true.

"Then who does?"

"What?"

"Who knows where Tristen is? One of you bastards has to know." Hope flirts with the vampire's black eyes.

"I might know someone." Defeat slipping from the words.

"Who?" The blade pushes against the middle finger. "Who knows where Tristen is?"

"An old one. She, well, she was there."

"Where?"

"The club. But you didn't come in. Or did you? She set that little bitch up for me. Got me something I wanted. Said I would pay it back somehow. Get her in touch with someone. A danger to her. I didn't understand what she was talking about. She's nuts. Like all the old ones. Only a really old vampire could do her any harm. But then there is you. Isn't there? A hunter of your caliber would worry one so old." The vampire's eyes look at the man with a sudden knowing. Jack's eye cocks. "She must have been talking about you. That's the only thing that makes sense. Because after I left, well here we are. She wants to meet you. I can get you in touch with her. I can call her. In my pants pocket. My phone." The head nods at the pocket beside its disfigured hand. The phone slips into Jack's hand, leaving the light cotton trousers. Jack presses the bottom that lights up the screen, then eyes the vampire questioningly.

"Pass code?"

"8543." Carlos blurts.

"Who should I be calling?"

"Ingrid."

"Alright." The light shines up at Jack as names scroll. Ingrid. Ringing, speaker on.

"Hello?" A slight German accent can be heard in the silvery voice.

"Ingrid." Desperation coming form Carlos.

"Ja?" Jack can hear the questioning tone.

Or is she toying with him? Jack wonders.

"It's me. It's Carlos." Desperation grows.

"Ah, what is it that you need?"

"I have what you want?"

"I doubt that, but what is it that you have?"

"The thing you said could hurt you?"

"You must be joking."

"No." Carlos is at a breaking point. He can see the malice in Jack's eyes. Like it is the sun burning into his skin.

"Alright, Carlos. I'm growing tired of your games. What is it you really want?"

"He wants to get through the night alive." Silence on the other end of the phone as Jack's voice cuts into the conversation.

"Whom may I be speaking to?" The girlish voice grows cold, the accent thickens.

"Not important."

"I assume you would like to meet? I assume that this is what this is about."

"Yes."

"Very well. Do you know the coffee shop in PB? The one the hippies go to."

"Yes."

"Tomorrow night, just after dark. Sit outside. I will find you. I do know what you look like Mr. Simpson." Question flashes over Jack's face then disappears. The phone darkens. The call is over.

"So. You can let me go." Glee bursts from the vampire. Jack leans down, the vampire's eyes try to follow. Fear widens them. A scream. Silence.

"God, I thought you'd never shut up." Jack steps back from the table. The stake sticking out of the vampire's heart. The scream frozen on the creature's face. Jack chuckles.

"You should see yourself, vampire. You look like a bad photo." He steps away from the table. His boots thumping on the concrete, echoing slightly in the newfound silence. A smile touches his lips. He pushes a button beside the door. A grinding of metal on metal, then a smooth-rolling sound. Predawn light floods the basement. A garden of wild roses bars the view of prying eyes. But not enough to block the suns rays from slipping into the room.

"I have to get going now, vampire. Have a pleasant day." He can see the vampire's eyes moving frantically. Fear has overcome it.

I'll clean up before I meet this Ingrid. He thinks as the

sound of his boot squeaks on the first step. The metal door swinging shut behind him. Carlos' eyes widen as sunlight grows bright against the opposite wall. Moving slowly toward him. A creeping death he cannot stop.

Chapter 4
Ingrid

ORANGE BLANKETS THE WESTERN SKY. THE SUN SINKS into the blue-green waters of the Pacific Ocean. Jack looks out at the few surfers catching the last waves of the day.

This better pay off. The thought runs behind the hard expression.

A group of college kids gather below him. The sound of laughter brings a scowl to his face. Pleasant things tend to do that to him now.

I used to be happy. His eyes watch the teens piling pallets into a concrete ring, the sand muffling their footfalls. *I used to be like them. Free. Free of the knowledge that monsters, the ones they tell you about in stories. The ones that are supposed to make kids do the right thing. That all that make-believe is not so make-believe after all.*

The sound of sneakers hitting the sandy sidewalk pulls his eyes in the direction of the sound. A man, late forties, in good shape. Runs with a youthful woman. College-aged. Pretty.

That could be me. With my daughter, if I'd had one. But Tabitha couldn't have kids. His blue eyes drift down to the cheap watch. *It's time.* He thinks as the sun slips below the waves. The last sparkle of safety shines on his t-shirt clad back.

Leaving the boardwalk for the backstreet that leads the main road that runs parallel the shoreline. He strolls among the beachgoers on their way home. Men, women, young, old. All shapes, sizes, and colors. Friendly and not so friendly faces. A child cries. Something about not wanting to leave. Jack moves through the crowd, waits for the light to change. A girl, maybe ten, drops her ice cream. A man laughs, drunkenness in his cruelty. The sadness in the girl's eyes touches Jack, reminds him of his own pain.

What I went through is nothing like a lost ice cream. His face turns to the green light, joins the crowd. Boots on asphalt. The chain diner already has a line to get in. Cheap food.

But I always liked the cheap stuff. It was Tabatha that liked it fancy. The higher-end restaurants, plays, opera. Not my thing. But she did love them.

He passes a club, the doors have been open since this morning. Bikini-clad girls and board-shorted boys drink to the sounds of the latest pop stars. His eyes take them in. The party atmosphere. Makes the sadness he carries with him sink deeper into his burdened heart.

Then then coffee shop can be seen. He can make it out. On the other side of the street. The outdoor seating is empty. He crosses, passes the gaggle of teens, and into the coffee shop. It's open. Chairs and tables of no similarity mingle on the sealed concrete floor. An old woman stands at the counter. She's poor. Jack can tell. The girl is smiling at her. The kind of smile that says sorry, but no. Jack's eyes scan the room. A middle-aged man sips a coffee. The untouched pastry sits on the table in front of him. A pair of girls are working on some kind of homework. The boy that hopes that one of the girls will notice him sits shyly two tables away. A couple of girls from the gaggle steps behind Jack. Giggling and silly from their day in the sun.

"Are you in line?" The politeness stuns Jack. He smiles kindly.

"Yes."

"Oh, it's going to be a while. Old Mary is trying to get some old stuff." The other girl sighs. Her hip juts out, eyes roll.

"What do you mean?"

"She comes in every day to get the throwaway stuff. She's not bad, just poor. I think she's homeless." The first girl says with the compassion that her friend lacks. Jack steps behind Mary. A youthful girl, blonde and pretty sits at a back table watching him. He watches her out of the corner of his eye, but she returns to her book. A vampire novel. He laughs inside at the irony.

"Excuse me." The gravel from Jack's voice brings the clerk and Mary's eyes on him. "What is it she needs?"

"Mary, you're going to have to step aside now. The stale stuff isn't ready for another hour." The clerk in her yoga pants and an 'I write books' tee says with a politeness that Jack wouldn't have expected. Mary steps away, mumbling something about hunger. Jack looks up at the chalkboard menu above him. "What'll it be?" The voice is pleasant, friendly. Yet there is a tinge of sadness there.

"Black coffee. You have a sandwich plate. What comes with that?"

"Drink, chips, and the sandwich you want. Would you like that? And what sandwich?" The girl's slender finger taps in the order. Then she looks up at Jack's face.

"Whatever Mary likes. Make sure she gets it. Poor folk need to eat too." Jack's tone is friendly, though the words shock the clerk. A smile grows on her face.

"Thank you." The happiness in her words is real, Jack can sense it. "She's a nice lady. Just had a lot of bad luck."

"I'll take that coffee now though." Jack's words are firm. The clerk smiles, she can tell that he's not looking for the good guy treatment.

"That'll be ten fifty." The clerk says and Jack slips a pair of twenties across the counter.

"Split the tip with Mary. She'll need to eat again." The girl makes change. The tip is put in a brown paper bag with a bag of potato chips.

"She needs it more than me. I got my rent for the month." The clerk nods as she brings the coffee.

Jack steps away from the good deed, coffee in hand. A line is forming. Young and old alike. He steps out into the cooling summer air. The smell of the ocean that never really goes away here. At least this close to the shore. He finds a stool. It faces the sidewalk. Party seekers are taking the place of the sun worshipers. He keeps a stool reserved.

The vampire should be here soon. The teens take the other end of the little patio.

More a strip, than a patio. Jack thinks as the stools are claimed. *So this is how you meet vampires. In coffee shops, surrounded by humans.* Jack's head moves slowly as his eyes take in the crowd in front of him. The swimsuits becoming nightlife attire.

"Hello." The silvery voice from the phone greets him. Jack turns. The girl from the table, the reader. She's behind him. The book hangs in the delicate hand, porcelain and petite.

Cute, a vampire reading about vampires. And the romantic notation too. She smiles, hypodermic fangs behind the painted red lips.

Pale blue eyes, the curiosity and the age shows in them. He turns, his larger frame facing her tininess. The fourteen-year-old body, if that old, stares up at him, though he is still seated on the barstool. Yet he knows that the fragile looking girl is more dangerous than he could ever be in a straight fight.

"You must be Ingrid." His hand moves slowly, cautiously to the stool beside him. The girls, just out of hearing, watch with cat-like curiosity.

"Thank you." Ingrid's form slips onto the stool, her sundress barely moving in the motion. A vampire trick of smoothness that humans have no ability for. She straightens the dress, girlish, playful. "I am glad to finally meet you, Mr. Simpson. It has been a while since a human has piqued my interest. You have made quite the name in my circle of, well, friends I guess you could call them. A man like you. Moving through the night. Killing vampires without concern or fear. Doing so at night, not hiding behind the sun and her protection. No, Mr. Simpson, you are a very interesting human being."

Her body shifts, her head turns, the girls watching look away. Blushing cheeks huddle in secret conversation. Ingrid's gaze returns to the hunter beside her.

"So, if you know about me and what a threat I am, then why the talk?"

"As I said, you interest me. And you did me a favor, not that you did it for me. More of a happy coincidence." The smile returns, this time with a touch of evil attached to it.

"That being?"

"Carlos. The vampire that you washed down the drain this morning."

"What about Carlos?"

"It was I that fed you the information that brought you to him. I lured him to take the girl, knowing you would be waiting. I also know that you are looking for another vampire. A powerful ancient. Older than I am." Her grin remains, but it is colder somehow. More dangerous, even in the crowd of the beach nightlife.

This can go bad fast. Jack reminds himself, using his eyes to find the enemies in the crowd. A man. A monster really, leaning against the storefront. The bathing suit-clad mannequins behind him. This man stares at the conversation. Watching, waiting for a sign. Ingrid follows Jack's eyes. Turns back to him.

"That would be Mario. He is a bit of a beast I must

say. But that is what makes him such a good bodyguard. He will not disturb us unless you become unruly."

"I see."

"I would think so. As I was saying. You rid me of Carlos. You see, he was becoming a nuisance. His killings were sloppy. Bringing attention that my kind do not need. Police attention. You solved that. Though, I have to admit it was cruel. Letting the sun kiss his delicate flesh. Still, we all have a manner of doing things. Yours is hard."

"What do you want?"

"I want nothing. You have given me what I want, as I have said. No, it is what I have that you want. That is why we are here. The vampire. The one you seek. I know his location."

"And? That could have been told over the phone."

"I wanted to see you. See the hunter that is sowing so much fear in my little community of bloodsuckers." Her laugh is a jingle of bells. Her head cocks slightly, flirtatious. The book waves slightly as she winks at the silliness of what it contains. "You didn't think my joke was funny. Unfortunate."

"Where is Tristen?" Jack's voice remains calm as the anxiety rips through him.

"That will come soon enough. First, I want to tell you I am surprised by you. A great vampire hunter. The kindness you showed that beggar woman. It shows character. Worth. And I assume you know something about me."

"Yes."

"Tell me. What is the word on the street, as they say."

"You don't kill. You limit killing among those that worship you."

"Worship is too strong a word. Follow is better. And yes, I do not kill. I learned that a vampire can survive on a small drink. One that neither kills nor turns the devotee. With the knowledge of drawing blood, storing it, well a vampire could live off that forever. A steady supply that harms no human life. You see, Mr. Simpson, I am what you would call a vegan among my kind. Yes, I need blood to survive. It is how I get that blood that makes me different. My followers have come to depend on the same method."

"And Carlos?"

"He was never one of my followers. A rogue, if you will. He was tolerated as a favor to Tristen. You see, we old ones do not take kindly to having our fledglings killed. And Tristen is very old. Now, I can see you are growing impatient. And it was kind of you to let an old woman rattle on. So I will give you what you have been looking for all this time. Since that horrid affair."

"Yes?"

"What you are looking for, and I would rather not name it, is in New York. The Paradise Hotel. I do not have the room number, though it would be convenient if I did. This hotel is in a seedy part of the city. Not that you will find an issue blending in." Her girlish smile returns. She winks. "And with that, I will be going. I do need to feed." The girlish figure slips to the concrete. Petite hands straighten the sky blue dress, adjust the left strap, pull back the blonde hair. She winks again. "Maybe we will meet again Mr. Simpson. I find you quite interesting. And as a final gift. I will be looking after the beggar from now on. She has some issues. Mental illness I believe that is what they call it in this age. I too have kindness within me."

The vampire in girls' form floats past the growing crowd. Jack's eyes follow her as she greets the beast standing in front of the mannequins. She smiles again as she slips into the back of a Mercedes. Jack leans back, the tension leaving him.

First time for everything. He thinks as the car containing the vampire that runs San Diego merges into traffic, then disappears to the east. *Now to get to New York… and Tristen.*

Chapter 5
Armand

THE JET'S ENGINE WHINES DOWN AS THE SUN GLARES through the porthole window beside Jack. Beside him, a woman, her knuckles bloodless and as pale as the vampires he hunts loosens her grip. Color returns to the fingers, she smiles with a nervous giggle.

"I hate flying." Her pouty mouth stumbles over the words. "It's all those movies and shows. The crashes. Like the one with that, God, I don't remember." Jack's eyebrow raises.

He nods. Others are standing in the little aisle. Reaching for the luggage above them. A suitcase sweeps past the woman's head, hair tossed by the wind. She reaches under her, pulls a small bag from in front of her, brings it to her lap. The uncertain smile returns. She moves up, falls back into the chair, giggles, and stands.

"My legs are a little woozy." The giggle is cute.

Jack nods, his face growing stern. Her smile disappears. She looks away, reddened cheeks glowing. Stiff legs take her into the line of travelers, never to see Jack again. He watches the line dwindle, thin, then almost disappear before he stands. He steps into the aisle, moves back, grabs a battered gym bag, and walks to the exit. Heat from the tarmac's humid air slaps him in the face as he steps onto the exit ramp. The seal not what it should be. The quiet grows distant as the terminal lights hit Jack's blue eyes. Crowds mingle. Couples hug, kiss, enjoy each other's presence. A pang of pain twists in his heart. He feels the loss that only such exchanges bring. It's crowded, more people than he would like to be around. Jack moves through the crowd, shouldering those that are in the way, getting rude looks. Not caring. He glances at his watch. Ten thirty.

Plenty of time to get supplies and get to the hotel. His mind surmises.

He moves around baggage claim into the sweltering heat of the day. An overhang providing much-needed shade, some cooling, separates him from the glaring sun. His hand flies up. The yellow car squeals to a stop. A youth jumps out. He's in the back of the cab before the boy can get to the door. As boy slips behind the wheel, he twists in the worn seat. Jack can smell the air freshener and today's lunch. It hits the hunter's nose, bringing an unpleasant lurch to his stomach.

"Where too?" The driver's accent is Puerto Rican, so different from the Mexican ones that belongs to that skin tone in San Diego. Yet, a genuine smile beams out at Jack.

"Brooklyn. Rockaway and Newport." The boy's eyes widen.

There's fear there. Jack notices.

"You sure man. That's a rough neighborhood and you, well, don't have the right kind of tan for that part of town."

"I'm sure." Jack's deadpan tone ends the argument.

The youth shrugs, turns, and puts the car in gear. Honks blare as the boy pulls into traffic. Jack can feel his body move back into the seat as the peddle moves closer to the floor. He pulls out his phone. As the screen lightens, a message pops up.

Armand. His eyes move over the message.

> *Jack,*
> *Figured you'd be back in town soon. Look,*
> *swing by the place and get whatever you need.*
> *Have a really nice blade for you. See you soon.*
> *Girls too, if you want them.*
> *Armand*

Jack slips the phone into his pocket. His eyes drift out over the city.

New York. It's been a while. Jack's head leans back.

His eyes close. Todays anxiety slips away, as he breathes deep. He can smell of cheap car freshener and it annoys his nostrils. The quiet hum of the road settles him. The cabbie is humming, not sure what tune it is, Jack lets it go.

It'll be over soon. I'll have it done. Then what? Go back to work as a regular guy. After all I've seen. All I've done. No, there has to be more to it.

Jack's eyes open as his body lifts off the seat, coming forward in a lurch. His eyes take in a part of New York that the tourist avoid. A seedier part of the city cannot to be found. They're off the freeway. On the surface streets. Close to Armand's front. Like a junky getting near his dealer, Jack becomes anxious.

Jack's eyes squint from the glare on the window. The sun's mid-day travel. Black faces shamble through the uneven concrete. Boards hide the interiors that hold nothing. Nothing but the refuge of those that have been left behind by a world that offers reward for greed. That greed comes out in the boys on the corner. Tracksuits, baggy pants. A fashion statement in most places, but here a work uniform. A hollowed-out man mumbles something and a little cash is exchanged for a baggie of white rock. Others move through the street.

These are good people. The thought moves through Jack's mind as the baller helps the old woman get her bags across the street. *No matter what they may say. These people are good. Just poor.*

The cab passes the old woman and her helper. Pulls against the crumbling curb. A youthful face turns to face Jack. There is concern in the dark brown eyes. And fear.

"This is it. You sure you want to get dropped off here?" A crack in the cabbies voice, his eyes dart. Jack moves his hand into the driver's space, a fifty between his fingers.

"Yeah." He slips out of the car, gym bag in hand.

Dark faces look at him. Suspicion and what could be fear. A squeal of tires. The cab speeds off. Jack's work boots crush the weeds as he makes his way through the broken sidewalk. He knows where he is going. A half block away. His stroll is casual, the faces turn away.

Almost taking him in as belonging here, but he knows that some are watching. White men are not common in this neighborhood and they tend to bring suspicion to the residents. Jack stops, looks up at the convenience store sign. Dirty. Cheap. No windows. A pair of partial glass doors greet him. Plywood is poorly screwed to the bottom frame of one of them.

Rust drips from the door hinges, but they swing silently out into the street. A buzzer announces him. An old black man behind the counter looks up from today's paper. His face twists into disgust. Jack steps forward. The store is split into two aisles by a long double-sided shelf. Coolers line the left and back walls. More shelves on the right. The clerk sits beside the beer cooler.

"Jack." It's more of an accusation than a greeting. "Here to see Armand, are we?" The paper shuffles, folds and is set on the counter. Coffee is pulled to the mouth with a thick New York accent.

"Yeah."

"Does he know you are coming?" A sip of coffee, cold eyes on the hunter.

"Yeah."

"Alright then. Let me see if he's available." The phone receiver is gripped in a hand that has seen hard labor. It goes to the ear. "Got Jack Simpson out here." Sound from the phone, someone talking. They sound excited. Jack wonders if it's one of Armand's girls from the high pitch blasting out of the receiver. "Alright then. I'll let him in." The receiver is cradled in the old-fashioned phone.

The clerk moves his hand slowly under the counter. A click. Behind Jack the swish of the chip rack moving into the store. The clerk nods in the direction of the rack. Jack steps to it, pulls it open. Inside, the narrow passage is lit by naked bulbs that hang from wires.

This isn't to code. Jack thinks as he steps into the claustrophobic tunnel.

The chips swing back into place. The ring of his boots hitting the concrete echo against the drywall faintly. Another door stops him, he turns the knob. He can hear the sound of rap music as it assaults his ears. A heavy steel door is pulled into the corridor. Blinding Jack with the light beyond.

"Jaaaack." The high-pitched squeal that could be from a school girl getting something special hits him as he steps into the living-room-like space. A pair of couches sit facing each other. A long wooden coffee table between them. A large TV and a fluffy chair on either end. The thin, rat-faced man pushes the underage hooker off his lap. Jack lets his eye adjust to the light. A video is on the TV, another underage hooker lounges on the couch farthest from Jack. Neither girl looks excited to be there.

"Hello, Armand." The dryness of Jack's words doesn't phase the pimp's excitement.

"It has been so long since you and I have been able to chat. Vampires still getting killed?" The gleeful look in the eyes of the pimp makes Jack cringe inside.

"Yes. Vampires are still being killed." Jack's head nods slightly. Armand slinks toward Jack, the girl that was on his lap collapsing on the couch beside the other girl. Jack's eyes wander over the girls.

Young. He thinks. *Maybe fourteen.*

He takes in the red haired girl, her plump body of the

one that contrasts the anorexic blonde with the sunken eyes that has her head in the plump girl's lap. Jack's eyes return to the pimp. His small frame. The thinness is almost comical. Armand glances back at the girls, then at Jack.

"You like what you see?" The sneer sickens Jack.

"Not really. A little too young for me."

"Ah, but once they get their boobs, well that's all I need." Jack fails to repress a sneer as the pimp leers at the girls cuddling on the couch. Jack's face returns to the emotionless slab as the grinning pimp looks up at him. "And you can have them both for free if you would like. Say, a gift among friends."

"No thanks. I have to get going after I get some tools." Jack's eyes look over the pimp.

He wants something. He's always had a fascination with the supernatural, but this friend thing is new.

"Ah, the tools of a hunter." Armand spins on his heel.

A swish in his walk, feminine. His head turns back. Jack follows, the girls' eyes never leaving him. One blows him a kiss, then both giggle. Armand leads Jack through a hallway. Horror movie posters line the passage. The sound of his boots hitting the hardwood floor echoes slightly on the hard surfaces. His eyes adjust to the dimming light.

"What do you have for me?" The gravelly voice can barely be heard. The place has a silence to it that feels like it shouldn't be broken.

This is all new. The girls, the secret passages. Jack takes in the place, fists balled. Ready for an ambush.

"I like to make it feel, eh, spooky." Armands toothy grin beams at Jack. It makes the rat face more rodent-like.

"But the things you need are behind this door. I had to start locking them up. Precious metals and all. Some of the people around here would break-in. Steal my stash." The pimp shrugs as he punches in the security code beside a heavy steel door. A beep. The door swings into the hall. Armand pulls it toward him. Jack follows the pimp into the vault.

"You see, I have everything you may need." The toothy grin remains fixed on the rat face.

"I see." Jack's eye takes it in. The walls lined with daggers, swords, and pistols. Oak drawers sit under the wall displays. "You have more customers? This is a lot of stuff for one guy."

"I have been expanding. You are not the only hunter out there." Armand steps aside as Jack's larger frame moves to the back wall.

A dagger hangs below the short swords. Jack's fingers touch the blade, move up it sensuously. He hides the grin that is forming on his lips. It's small, easily hidden. Jack turns, looks at the pimp-turned arms dealer.

"How much for this one?"

"Five thousand for that one."

"Alright." Jack pulls a roll of hundreds from his pocket.

Counts them out and hands fifty of them to Armand. The dagger slips into Jack's boot, his loose jeans hiding it from curious eyes. Armand steps out of the armory with Jack behind him. The pimps thin arms pushing the steel door closes with a click, and Armand's nod tells Jack to follow. They pass the movie posters and enter the bright living room. The girls turn to look. They smile, trying to be sexy, coming off as young and stoned.

"Are you sure you don't want to stick around for a bit? It's going to get dark soon. Vampire hunting is always better left to the morning hours. Or so they say." Armand winks and nods to the girls. "They might not be old enough for you, but they are still old enough."

"No, I think I'll take my chances with the vampire now. I have plenty of daylight left." The slight growl in Jack's voice causes the pimp to shrug.

"Your loss. If you change your mind after the killing, come by. You can tell me all about it and we can have a little celebration."

"If I survive."

"It's Tristen." The pimp's eyes go wide. Realization smashing through the cheap grin. "The ancient one."

"Yes."

"You finally found him. The one that…" Jack's raised hand silences the pimp.

"Later. After I've finished it. I need to stay focused."

"Then, I hope you succeed. I truly hope you kill that monster." Armand presses a button on the wall. Silence. A questioning look from Jack.

"Willie needs to open the door. Make sure no one is wandering the store." Armand's thin smile is sad. "I hope I see you again. You are something special in this world. I know. I have asked around." The pop of the door on the other end of the line of light bulbs brings Jack back to the here and now. He moves quickly through the tunnel as the door swings into the store. Jack steps out among the chips, turns looks at Armand.

"Thanks, Armand. I hope to see you again too."

"As do I."

The door swings closed as Armand watches the hunter move out into the street.

"Yeah. Yeah, I know what neighborhood it is. But the guy needs a cab and you need to get someone to pick this white boy up. Alright, ten minutes. Good." Willie hangs the phone up. Looks at Jack leaning against the aluminum door frame.

Hope that asshole makes it through this. I kinda like his white ass. Willie thinks as he watches Jack loiter around the store.

Chapter 6
Jack

THE SMELL OF URINE AND SWEAT HITS JACK. HE LOOKS AT the peeling paint, the faded awning, the bled-out letters.

A strange place for an ancient. Jack's thoughts move through his mind as his body does on the sidewalk.

Bums sit on the steps, dozing in the summer heat. The sun, still high enough to light the city, to protect the hunter. Is beginning to dip behind the mid-rise buildings. Its rays fading.

I don't have much time. Need to get this over with. Bastard might already know I'm here or that I'm on the way. Can't trust that Ingrid. This can still be a setup. A trap laid out. The only reason to get me here. Tristen would never stay in a hole like this without a reason. And that would be getting me alone. To kill me. A dead body here wouldn't mean a thing.

Jack looks back. The cab that brought him here disappears into the traffic. The street, the afternoon bustle, leaves little room for movement.

"Got any change?" A dirty hand stretches out.

The eyes down, shamed. Jack pulls out a few bucks. Drops them into the beggar's hand. Looks at the others, shakes his head. A few put their hands out, mumbles of miscellaneous pleas. Jack ignores them, he has to get this done. The heat of the sun is still on him, but his legs are cooler. He steps over a sleeping leg. Pulls the grimy door toward him, lets the mold and body odors hit him. Stops the need to vomit and moves inside.

It's an ugly room. He thinks as his eyes wander the little lobby.

Bums linger on couches, corners, chairs. The carpet is worn through. Plaster and lathe showing on the nearly paint-less walls. Stairs, once grand, are now a sad remembrance of a past that is long gone. A cage, that's all that Jack can think that it can be, sits beside the stairs. A man. Small. Hair slicked back. Dirty shirt, half unbuttoned down his hairy chest. Beard hiding most of the crucifix that glitters gold. He sits behind the bars, a magazine in hand. Eyes look up, see Jack moving closer. The magazine drops to the counter.

"Whatcha want?" The sneer is arrogant. Arms held across the open shirt. Arm hair mingles with the chest. A cigarette smolders in a full ashtray. The stale smell of tobacco. Jack leans forward.

"Tristen."

"Can't help you, man." The magazine lifts off the counter. Jack's hand moves through the bars of the cage faster than the man can react. Jack has the man's beard, a shirt can rip. Fear forms in those arrogant eyes. "I can't give out guest info, man. It's policy."

"Don't care. I need to see the bastard now." Jack's arm jerks toward him.

The head slams into the cage. A trickle of blood. An unnatural bend to the clerk's nose.

"Room two thirteen, man." The clerk moves back, out of grabbing distance as Jack's arm moves onto the correct side of the cage.

"If you're lying."

"No, man. Just fuck off." The clerk coddles his nose, trickles of blood drip down to mix with the dirt on his shirt. Jack steps away. The stairs are in front of him.

Now I finish it. The anger boils inside him, pure hate. His first step toward revenge is taken on a rotting piece of wood. He stops at the top of the stair, looks back. The bums lounge. One drinks from a half-empty bottle.

Something's not right. It's too easy. Blue eyes scan the lobby. His stomach tightens. No one looks at him. Most doze. Others drink. None seem to care.

You're second-guessing yourself. Even old vampires fuck up. Now let's get this done before it gets dark. Jack ignores the lobby and that little voice warning him as he turns his eyes on the dim hall. Mildew and shit. The stench of piss. Holes show the rooms through crumbling walls.

How is this place even standing? His thoughts wander as the room numbers grow. Nine. Eleven. Thirteen. The door stands hard before him. Legs spread slightly. He listens. The sound of TV's and music from other rooms. Quiet from the one he stands before. His leg moves back, swift it moves to the door. Heel connects. The flimsy latch shatters. The door swings in on battered hinges. Jack's look of anger, hate, revenge fades. Shock and a lack of understanding wash over him. Two cops, guns are drawn, face him. Their barrels watching his every move.

"Don't even think about it asshole." A voice is behind him, by the stairs. Thick with heavy cigarette use. Jack freezes. The uniformed officers remain tense, fingers twitching on the triggers. Jack's eyes move toward the voice, head slowly following. A large, sloppy man with a cropped haircut and mustard on his shirt points a snub nose thirty-eight at Jack's chest. Beside him, a greying woman holds a nine-millimeter in the same direction. He shifts his foot, the uniformed cop's muscle tightens, he stops.

"Going to face the plainclothes cops." The gravel in his voice keeps the sound low, hard to hear. Tension lightens slightly in the fingers that press against the triggers. Jack moves his foot, shifts his torso at a crawl. Faces the detectives in front of him. Moves his hands into the air.

"Is there a problem officer?" He can't think of anything else, instinct, like being pulled over on the highway.

"This guy here." The slob chuckles. "Don't know if I like his mouth or want to smack it."

The greying woman moves swiftly. Faster than Jack expected. She gets behind him, her muscular hands gripping his elbows, pushing his face up against the lathe.

"Spread 'em." Her light voice growls.

She slips the cuffs around his wrists, face pressed into the splintering wood. The sound of clicking as his feet are kicked to the side. One of the uniforms holsters his pistol and moves behind Jack as the woman steps back. Rough hands move across his shoulders, over his chest, back the waist of his jeans, down to his crotch, then to his legs.

They stop at the boot, lift the cuff of his pants, he can feel the dagger pulling out of his boot.

"What's this?" The slob sneers at Jack, too close. Hot dog breath pelts Jack. He turns away. "Don't you look away from me punk?" His head jerks back, a thick hand in his hair.

"Your breath stinks." Jack growls. The slob stumbles as he moves away from the glaring eyes. "You should brush your teeth if you want to get that close to someone." The woman stifles a laugh, he can't see her, but he can feel her turning away.

"Fuck you buddy. This'll get you some time." The dagger turns in the man's hand.

"No, it won't."

"And busting into that room, well that's breaking and entering buddy."

"I was visiting a friend. Thought it would be funny to scare him is all. Asked what room he was in downstairs. Ask the clerk." Jack turns, his back leans against a hole in the wall. The slob's face reddens, he moves closer, eyes burning.

"You listen here."

"No, you listen. You don't have anything. If that isn't Tristen's room, then well, I made a mistake. Not a crime. And you still only go after criminals, right?" Jack watches the eyes of the slob become slits. He turns to his partner. A faint grin is on her lips.

"We talked to the clerk. You got a little rough. Could get you on assault." The greying woman's voice is calm. Her temper is steadier than the slobs.

"Yeah, well, he was a bit of an asshole." Jack shifts. *Not out of this yet.*

"Yes, he is. But the undercover cops witnessed it. Saw you manhandle him."

"What do you want?"

"Who said I wanted anything?"

"I'm not in the back of a car. That's who."

"Smart. I have a friend. She would like to talk to you."

"Talk?"

"Yes."

"Alright." Jack eyes the woman as she nods to one of the uniforms. He jogs to the stairs, the sound of his holster slapping on his leg competes with the straining wooden stairs. "What does your friend want?"

"She can tell you. She's not one to say much to us, *lackeys*." The detective laughs, eyes roll. Her partner growls something that Jack can't make out. The woman pulls Jack forward, removes his cuffs, smiles at him. "That's her there." The detective nods toward the stairs.

Jack's eyes look over the youth moving toward him. Her walk is cat-like. The business suit cut to fit her, tailored. The light, sky blue jacket, deep purple silk top, matching skirt that comes to her knees hiding the thin frame. The mousey bob cut bouncing as her leather heels glide across the musty carpet. She stops in front of Jack, looking up at him. An air of superiority.

"Good afternoon, Mr. Simpson." Curt, to the point. No emotion in the words. A musical note to the voice, attractive. Easy to listen to. He would guess her a vampire if not for the time of day.

"What do you want?" Jack watches her. The face a porcelain mask.

The detectives shuffle toward the stairs. The woman looks back, shakes her greying hair, and disappears down the creaking wood.

"My name is Abby Vinson. I've been asked to escort you to my office." The musical notes clash with the lack of emotion.

What an odd way of speaking, pretty but distant. Like a song heard on a radio turned too low or just at the end of range. Jack thinks.

"You set me up." Feet planted, his arms held across his chest, shirt bunching. His eyes simmer as he looks at the girl's pale brown eyes. Her head turns to the side, questioning his words with movement.

"Yes." Blunt. Hard. The words almost shock him.

"Why?"

"We need your talents. My superior will explain." The same monotone.

So she is the errand girl. Jack realizes.

"And if I refuse?"

"I can have the detectives detain you. Until such time as you are willing to comply." The questioning head turns.

She doesn't get people. She can't read me. She's not used to someone refusing her requests. Not spoiled though, something else, almost military-like. Robotic.

"And where is it that I am supposed to go?"

"The exact location will be revealed soon. Until then you must trust me."

"You just set me up."

"Not I. But I see you are not sure what is in store for you. Let me be clear. You are being persuaded to come with me. Meet with my superior. Answer some questions and then it is your decision whether you remain. The setup, as you would say, is to get the meeting. Not to imprison you."

"Alright. What is it exactly you need?"

"As I said, that will be explained…"

"By your superior. Fine. Lead the way."

Chapter 7
Carol

THE GLARE OF THE WINDOWS OPPOSITE JACK BLINDS HIM as the stench of the lobby is left behind for the smell of car exhaust from the street. Squinting eyes get past the reflected light to reveal a black town car sitting in the loading zone. The chauffeur, at attention, stands beside the open door. The pixie of a woman leads him toward the car. Her silence is comforting. Jack remains a pace behind her, letting his eyes take in the lithe form. She is in good shape, strong. An athlete's build. She moves past the sleeping bodies with the grace of a gymnast.

This one trains. She turns her round face toward the hunter, looks him in the eyes. *There's no fear there.*

"You asked me about what my superior wants of you. That I cannot tell you, Mr. Simpson. What I can explain, is what our organization is. In broad terms."

The cold face disappears with the rest of the woman's body into the back of the town car. A nod from the driver tells Jack he is to follow. The hunter slips onto the black leather seat, it's smoothness providing little friction against his jeans. Abby sits. Legs crossed at the ankles, hands placed lightly on her lap. Reminding Jack of a schoolgirl. The door closes silently, the sounds of the street disappear. A plate of glass separates the pair from the driver as he takes the wheel. The feel of the engine, slight but there, and the car pulls into traffic. Jack looks at the youthful woman, almost a girl in his eyes.

"What is it that you do?" His body twists toward her, eyes focused on the face that looks out at traffic. She turns to face him. Emotionless as the feminine form angles itself toward him.

"We are an ancient order." The tone is soft, but there is a firmness there. Telling Jack not to interrupt. He remains silent as the girl's monologue slips between her red lips.

"During the Renaissance, a group of scholars discovered that some of the myths were true. Vampires, werewolves, ghosts. All of this existed in the shadows of our own society. Some, like vampires, needed to hunt among us. Needed to feed on human prey. Others, werewolves, for example, had little need for human contact and tended to keep to the edges of human civilization. It was these creatures that brought scholars together. These works were discarded as foolishness by universities, as they are now." Her eyes looked at the hunter, the grimness of his features. "Does this make sense, Mr. Simpson?"

"So far."

"Good. The few scholars that began to understand what humanity faced continued their work in secret. Working together they formed The Society. A simple term designed to give no clue to the actual ideals that those that belonged held. Of course, there have been secret handshakes, and signs over the centuries. Much like other secret societies. We have left those behind us now, as you will learn if you wish to remain with us."

"So you study monsters?"

"In a sense, yes. We observe and track them. We learn about them and what can be done to stop them."

"And you do nothing to stop them." A sneer sweeps over Jack's lips.

"That is not entirely true. We do seek out the worst. Put an end to them. We seek to keep the population low."

"But not to eradicate."

"That is not our place."

"Why?"

"I don't understand."

"Why is it not your place?" Jack's heated words contrast with the calm of the girl's controlled speech.

"The Society was not formed to be a warrior cult. Designed to seek out and destroy the supernatural. We are observers. We gather information. That is our purpose."

"While the supernatural hunts down and destroys mankind."

"Yes."

"I'm not sure if you are any better than the creatures you observe." Venom drips from the words as Jack turns, looking out at the darkening street. At the masses in their business suits and high-end fashion walking along the Manhattan sidewalks. The stores, restaurants, bars.

How can this girl admit that this group of hers knows of the horrors that face these poor saps and do nothing to stop it.

Population control. Funny. It has to be eradication. An end to the species that would end humanity.

"Mr. Simpson. We are in agreement on the lack of will that my organization shows in stopping the supernatural threats that we face." Jack turns, looks at the granite face. Eyes facing out into the street. Watching the taillights. Holding whatever emotion there may be inside.

Something happened to her. This is the behavior of a trauma victim.

"What else can you tell me?" The words come out softer. He feels a shared pain with this girl now, something that they have in common.

"These creatures." A slight tremor in her voice. It confirms his hypothesis. "They are increasing. It was not always the case. For decades after the industrial revolution, they were on the decline. Numbers plummeted. Scholars did not know why. Possibly the pollution, but no clear answer. This continued into the nineties. Then the populations began increasing, again there is no clear answer for why. It seems that whatever caused the decrease disappeared or they adapted. But it didn't make sense, as it affected all of the supernatural creatures. It was then that The Society decided it had to act. It created hunters, like yourself, to provide a means of population control. But this is not an easy task. Most do not last long."

"Now I see why you need me."

"Possibly. I have not been told why your presence is desired. In this case, I am simply doing an errand. I know nothing about you, Mr. Simpson, only that you are needed by the order and that it is of great importance. If I could tell you more, I would."

Jack closes his eyes, lets the girl's words sink in. *I need to be careful around these people. Rumors about these groups. Most of them nuts. Fanatics some of them. But the girl seems together. Have to see how it works out.* His mind drifts to thoughts of happier times, before the knowledge of the supernatural, before vampires became real. This city flies by the tinted glass. His eyes grow heavy.

✳ ✳ ✳

"Mr. Simpson, we are here." The silvery voice wakes him.

Shouldn't have done that. Didn't think I was that tired, but I should have stayed awake. Crap. Jack rubs the sleep out of his eyes.

It's dark. The smell of the country hits him as the door opens. The driver steps away, the black suit blending into the darkness that the oaks beyond create. A whinny.

Horses. Of course, they have horses.

Abby moves around the blackness that separates her from Jack. Tail lights turn her a ghostly red, then back to the pale girl he met in the hole of a hotel.

"Where are we?" Soft light glows gently from the windows, large windows, onto a wide porch that wraps the building. Wooden rocking chairs, tables, and low benches sit welcoming. The dark doesn't hide the shape of the two-story mansion, the Greek revival style. The large door, designed to make the visitor feel small in comparison. The damp of the air raises bumps on his skin.

"It is one of our hubs." The girl says as Jack eyes her.

Small hands straighten the skirts slight wrinkles in the light material. Hair pushed back behind her ears, small ears that have trouble doing the job of a hair tie. His eyes return to the mansion. Looks old, but it's not. Built in the eighties from the materials that were used. His eyes drift back to hers.

"Hubs?"

"Yes. A place where members can gather. Discuss research. Learn from each other. Add to the archives."

She looks like I should know this. She's been here most of her life. Maybe all of it. She doesn't get the world outside of this place. Outside of these people. Jack nods politely as the girl moves gracefully toward the wide steps that lead to the massive oak door.

"Is this where you live?"

"Yes." *That was too blunt. She doesn't want to talk about it. I may have hit a nerve. Strange.*

"And your superior is here?"

"Yes, and she is expecting you."

"Alright." Jack nods, letting it sink in that these people did not expect her to fail. That they knew he would come. *This has been planned out. Crafted. At least they think things through.*

Gravel crunches under the tires, Jack looks over his shoulder to see the red glare slowly disappear around a corner of the house. His head returns to the girl. Her hand pulling the massive door open with ease. A warm glow greets them. The smell of wood. Smoke from a fire. A homey smell. Inviting. The click of Abby's heels on the marble floor brings Jack's attention to the foyer. Veins of black in the white of the floor. Joints nearly invisible. Light oak wainscoting with an off-white plaster above. An oak stair twisting to the second floor, the modern pendant light hanging from a delicate chain, the wiring braided within.

Money. Jack takes it in. Looks at the girl standing, arms folded across her petite chest. Emotion missing from her features.

"My superior is this way." The flat words. The girl's cat-like movement into the darker hall. Can lights, the bulbs too low, throw shadows between each fixture.

Creepy place. They turn, then again, then again. *The place is a maze.*

She stops. A pair of oak doors, matching the wainscoting end the hall. Abby turns. Looks at the hunter. Attempts a smile and fails. A light rap on the wood.

"Come in." The voice is confident, aged. The sound of years of cigarette smoke and hard drink has had a toll on the vocal cords. Abby opens the door. Light floods into the hall. A woman faces Jack. Her hair greyed with the eighty-some years of life. A light jacket covers the white blouse. Pearls frame the saggy flesh. Bright eyes look at him. A subdued brown. His own eyes move to the girl. Same eyes. He looks back. The woman has risen from the overstuffed leather chair. Light shining on its chocolate color. The men on either side remain seated, uninterested.

She's the master here. Jack determines.

Jack steps forward. An empty chair in between him and the oak coffee table. The woman on the other side of the tea service, a silver pot glittering on the light oak.

"Mr. Simpson." Jack can tell it's a statement from the old woman.

The men stand, one glares with almost black eyes. His own jowls shake slightly as his thin, almost skeletal frame steps to a side door. The other, the one with a bloated stomach and ruddy face smiles, nods, and exits behind his thinner counterpart. A click of the door and the woman nods to Abby as she stands behind Jack. Slight breeze and the door behind him clicks. They are alone.

"Please, have a seat, Mr. Simpson." The old woman's liver-spotted hand motions to the chair opposite her. Jack slips around the chair, settles into the softness, lets the leather cushion him. Her smile makes him grimace.

"What is it you want?" A growl drips out of the distorted mouth.

"Coffee?" She lifts the silver pot with grace, the black liquid flows with ease into the porcelain cup. The pastel roses breaking up the white.

"No, thank you." His voice is firm, but there is no malice in it. The old woman leans back, her eyes taking him in. His stomach tightens.

"Polite. From our reports that was not to be expected. But you are educated, are you not?" Cup touches wrinkled lips. The black liquid within passing between them.

"Yes."

"And what might that be? What exactly is your education, Mr. Simpson?"

"I'm sure you know."

"Humor me, Mr. Simpson. What is it that you studied?"

"Architecture."

"And did you become an architect? Or was is just schooling?"

"I have my license to practice."

"I see. It was then that the unfortunate event occurred."

"You could say that."

"Then you went out into a world that was only make-believe before."

"Yes."

"Became one of the most feared hunters of our time."

"Sure, if you say so."

"It is not me saying so. Ingrid was certain of it."

"The vampire?"

"Yes. Don't let her age deceive you. She is over five hundred years old. Born in Germany, well it wasn't called that then, but none the less that is where she was turned. She finds that killing humans is distasteful."

"So she says."

"It is true."

"Why are you working with a vampire?" Jack's patience is slipping.

"No, you misunderstand. We do not work with vampires. In this case, Ingrid and this organization have a common enemy. We will work together to defeat this enemy. Then we will part ways."

"What enemy?"

"Another vampire. Close, but the location is not known. At least not to us. Nor too Ingrid. No, Mr. Simpson, that is where you come in. This is why I have asked that you be brought to us."

"Find the vampire?"

"Yes. Then destroy it."

"What's in it for me? I have a vampire I'm looking for. Don't need another one."

"We know where Tristen is."

"Where?"

"That will be revealed after you have taken care of our problem."

"Find a vampire that you can't find and kill it."

"Yes."

"You don't have hunters?"

"Not of your caliber."

"Alright. What do you have?"

"Very little, unfortunately. I will provide you with a dossier. It contains the limited information that we have. It is a start."

"When can I see it?"

"As soon as we are finished. But there are other items that needs to be discussed."

"Such as?"

"My niece."

"The girl you sent."

"Very receptive of you."

"You have the same eyes. Similar features."

"I see. She is to assist you in this hunt."

"No."

"No?"

"No."

"Then it seems we do not have a deal. Her coming along, learning from you is one of the few reasons we chose you. If you refuse, there are other options. And no Tristen." Jack gazes into the brown eyes. This is not a bluff.

"Alright. She can come. She needs to do as I say."

"Excellent."

"If she dies?"

"You will not be held responsible."

She's lying. The girl dies, I get nothing.

"I'd like to look over that dossier now."

"Very well. Abby is waiting for you at the door. She can have something brought to you."

"Brought to me?"

"Dinner, Mr. Simpson. I believe that you haven't eaten since this morning. You must be hungry."

"Sure." Jack nods, the emptiness of his stomach comes to his thoughts as he stands.

The woman remains seated, refilling her cup. It is clear to him that he has been dismissed. Jack stands, looks at the old woman and turns to the door. The sound of his boots on the marble breaks the silence. His hand turns the nod, the door swings toward him. He looks at the girl standing in the shadows, waiting.

"I look forward to you resolving this complication for us." There is a relief in the old woman's words. More relief than Jack would have thought.

"And I look forward to Tristan's location."

Chapter 8
Jack

"ARE YOU HUNGRY, MR. SIMPSON?" THE SILVERY VOICE without emotion asks from a slightly tilted head. It reminds Jack of a puppy, one aiming to please.

Or is that just in my head? Because I'm supposed to train her. Teach her to be a killer like me. He thinks as the oak door closes off the old woman from his curious eyes.

"Yes. And you can call me Jack. Mr. Simpson is too formal for our line of work." The tilt of Abby's head grows closer to her shoulder, a glimmer of a smile, just barely there. Then gone. "What do they have?"

"The chef can provide anything you like."

"A sandwich would be fine and coffee. It'll be a late night."

"Oh?"

"The dossier." His brow bunches in the middle. Something's missing. Something not made clear by the old woman.

"I see. I'm afraid you will be disappointed. There

is little within. Notes mainly. That will be clear soon enough, come I'll show you to your room. What kind of sandwich would you prefer?"

"I'm not too picky. Surprise me." A shadow becomes a youthful man. Reddish hair. Acne. A nervous smile, but not because of Jack. The smile is directed at the girl. *A crush.* Jack smiles inside as he follows the girl. His head turns over his shoulder. The boy disappears around a corner of the maze of hallways.

"He likes you." Jack breaks the silence as the pair move through the labyrinth.

"Yes." She stops, turns, looks him in the eye. "I do not have an interest in him." The cold of her tone chills even his hard exterior.

"Oh." The hunter's eye cocks as her deadpan expression remains. Her hand turns the brass nod of the oak door. It swings open. Jack stands firm.

"He is an intern. Learning his craft. I am not. It would not be proper to be involved with him." Her hand motions to the interior of the room.

She likes him too. It's the aunt that holds her back. Jack realizes.

"Alright. And the dossier?"

"On the bed. Anthony will bring your sandwich shortly. I have some last-minute items to attend to." She turns. The sound of her clicking heels disappears around another corner.

I embarrassed her. He laughs to himself as he steps into the darkness, finds the switch, and lightens the small room.

It is a dorm room. His eyes take it in. Single bed

with a dark blue wool blanket. A small desk under a small window. Wooden chair in front of it. The night sky shining down on him. A door that he assumes leads to a closet. The floor is carpeted, it muffles his steps. The dossier sits on the bed. All too thin.

"Let's see what they have?" His hand takes the dark brown folder off the bed. Opens it, finds a typed report within.

She wasn't kidding. Not much here at all. Some notes from a Garfield.

Jack's eyes scan the first page. Stats on the vampire he's looking for. Height, weight, apparent age, actual age, hair, etc. All basics. No substance.

This isn't much to go on. He flips the sheet over. *Ah, a bio. This might help. This Garfield has a write-up on her.*

For Society Use Only:

Memo: The vampire Marie.

> *The vampire is of unknown origin, though it is believed that she is from a nordic country and immigrated to the United States some time ago, as her accent is very slight. She is of medium height, though actual height has not been determined. Eye color could not be determined due to sunglasses being worn.*
>
> *The Society was approached by said vampire and given a dossier. Said dossier provided information on the organization and locations of safe houses throughout the world as well as information on high-ranking members.*

Vampire asked that she and her group be given special status. She wanted to be free of possible eradication by The Society. In exchange, the Societies 'secrets' would be safe from other vampires that would surely wish to use them for more 'nefarious' means. The Society promised to not use its members to hunt the vampire in question. Said vampire returned to whatever location it had come from, believed to be upstate New York.

This member recommends that something should be done to neutralize this threat, as the vampire is more than likely to sell Society information at some point in the future. Possibly an outside, freelance hunter so said vampire could not identify any current hunters being assigned to her. I believe that said vampire has access to the Societies network. As such I have typed this on an old typewriter and handed the file to my superiors without entering it into the network.

Note, there is one clue to the identity of the said vampire. A young fledgling that has recently been seen working the punk rock bars for victims. I am not sure if this young vampire left on her own or if she was removed from the coven for some discretion. See attached bio on fledgling.

The folder closes slowly in the hunter's hand. He looks at it. Disappointment takes over his expression. The folder drops onto the desk. He looks out at the stars, his mind working.

The fledgling is the key. I need to get to her. Get the location of the one that turned her. I need Jeff. He's not going to like this.

Jack spins to see the door of his room slowly moving into the space.

"Mr. Simpson." The cracking voice and the acne-covered face relaxes him. The boy stands waiting.

"Come in." Jack sits on the bed as the boy's thick form enters. Jack's sandwich sits on a silver tray. Bottled water beside it. The boy smiles, sets the tray on the desk, looks at the hunter.

"You're a hunter." The cracking voice leaves the boys body. Jack chuckles inside as the boy's face reddens, eyes at the carpet.

"Yes. Why?"

"I haven't seen too many. They come in sometimes. Stay a night and then disappear."

"It's demanding work." Jack takes the sandwich off the porcelain plate. His teeth sink into the ham and cheese. A hint of mayo and mustard. The tart of tomato.

"Can I ask you something?" The tip of the boy's shoe strokes the carpet with nervous energy, reminding Jack of a small child.

"Sure." Jack answers around a mouthful of food.

"What's it like?"

"Killing vampires?"

"No, being alone all the time?" The boy's words strike at Jack. He leans back. The sandwich drops to his lap. The boy looks at him, eyes waiting for an answer.

"Lonely." Disappointment flickers across the boy's face.

"Oh."

"It's not for those that need others. It's not a glamorous life. Most of the people in your life will be distant. Because you will have to keep them safe."

"Even the ones you love?"

"Especially the ones you love. If a vampire, or any other creature, finds you are attached. In love. That you care deeply about someone or something. It puts them at an advantage. Better to be distant. Fewer funerals that way." The boy's eyes redden with a pain Jack doesn't understand. He turns. Shuffles to the door. Looks back.

"I don't know if I could live that way."

"No one can live that way, not really. It's more a burden than a lifestyle." The boy nods.

An understanding in his eyes. A sad smile moves across his lips. He steps out of the room, pulls the door closed, and leaves Jack to his solitude. Something the hunter has come to cherish and despise at the same time. He picks up the note, tosses the remains of the sandwich on the plate, and opens the little sheet of paper.

Mr. Simpson,

As I told you, and you have now discovered for yourself, there is very little in the dossier. I asked the chef to provide water with your meal. I will see you in the morning. Have a good night.

Yours,
Abby.

The note drops on the desktop. He pulls the blanket down, strips, and settles into bed.

This is a strange place. He thinks as his mind drifts off to sleep.

Chapter 9
Sal

SUNLIGHT WARMS JACK'S NAKED SKIN. HE LETS THE warmth soak in. His arm moves up, shielding his eyes from the light that tries to penetrate his eyelids. His nose wrinkles at the smell of his body. His arm moves. Eyes open to a pleasant room, so different from the dim light of the night before. Off-white walls, no wainscoting. Hardwood floor. The desk and chair, as he left them. The little closet door.

This place. It's so relaxing. I could lounge here all day. Just a book and a pot of coffee. His fingers grip the wool blanket, soft linen sheets beneath. They're pulled back, his nudity exposed to the empty room. Legs swing over the soft mattress. Ab's engaged and his body is upright.

I need a shower. I plain stink. He stands, steps over the pile of clothes on the floor, and walks to the closet. The brass nob turns easily, the silent swing of the door as it moves into the bedroom.

A small bathroom greets him. White tile floor. White

walls. Sunlight gives a warm glow from a wide window above the shower. He steps onto the cool floor, lets the sensation move through the sole of his foot. A click of the door to his room. He turns. A young woman is peering in, uncertainty on her face. He moves to the side, letting the wall shield his nakedness.

"I'm in the bathroom." The gravelly voice bellows.

"I was asked to come check on you, Mr. Simpson. See if you needed anything." A tremor of fear is in the light voice.

"Coffee. Black." Jack's voice softens. *You don't need to scare the girl. She's just a maid.*

"Would you like some clean clothes and breakfast?" The fear is gone in the girl's voice. The sound of her shoes stepping on the wood floor drifts to Jack's ears.

"Sure." A shuffle of clothes being scooped off the floor. The tip-tap of the girl's pace. The click of the door closing. His head looks out into the bedroom. His boots remain. The rest is with the girl.

I hope they bring something decent to wear. Not in the mood for slacks and a dress shirt.

Jack's attention returns to getting clean. He looks in the mirror. The blonde stubble. The refreshed eyes. All that he needs is laid out in an orderly fashion on the sink. He starts with the razor.

This girl. Abby, I think that's right, she is to follow me around. Learn my ways. And this aunt of hers. There is something there. Something she's not telling. Something about that girl. She's damaged inside. Like me. She's lost someone, something that is close to her. Her parents maybe. A sibling. And why is she here? She hinted at being here for a time. It's not what you'd call child-friendly. Jack looks over the shave, takes the toothbrush, adds paste, and works on his teeth. *And this Marie. What does this vampire have on them? And Ingrid? They are working together to destroy her. Odd. Humans and vampires don't mix well.*

Jack rinses his mouth, moves to the shower. The water warms, he gets in. The heat soothes his muscles. *Didn't realize I was sore. New bed.* He lathers, washes, dries. *There's more going on here than they're letting on.*

Movement in the bedroom. He stops. Ears on alert. A shuffling sound. The clanking of metal on metal. He wraps the towel around him. Steps into the bedroom. Abby sits on the made bed. A teen girl sets fresh clothes beside her. Jack looks at the young woman. She smiles.

"If there is nothing else miss." The voice from before. The girl disappears out into the maze of hallways. Jack turns to Abby. She pours coffee, steam rising from the black liquid, into a pair of mugs. So unlike the elegance of the night before. The pot is stainless, the mug's ceramic. The plain dark blue color of the mugs are attractive to the eye.

"I believe we have a busy day ahead of us, Jack." He smiles inside as she says his name. A lack of confidence as she does so.

"I need to get dressed first. Unless you would prefer me in a towel." The evil grin touches the corner of his mouth.

"Yes, that may cause undue attention. I will step into the hall." Red grows on her face.

She's embarrassed. Emotion. That's a first.

"Sure. Are we going to talk in here?"

"Yes." The reddened face looks at him. Eyes drift to the hand on the towel. Eyes widen slightly, her head turns away. She stands. A quick pace takes her into the hall.

"I don't think she's seen a naked man before." His chuckle is low, unheard by the girl beyond the door.

Jack's head shakes slightly as he pulls the jeans from the bed. The kind he likes. The tee has a punk band print on it. *They have been watching me. For some time. They know my style. And I know nothing about them. I'm at a disadvantage here.*

The clothes slip on quickly. Perfect fit. He sips the black coffee, leaving the one with cream on the desk. His eyes look at the closed door. *Who are these people?*

"I'm dressed if you want to come in." His voice booms. The door opens, Abby steps in. The redness disappearing. The cat-like grace returning. She straightens her slacks, sits on the bed. At the foot. Where the clothes had been. She looks up, takes the coffee Jack holds out to her.

"Thank you." The silvery voice has a timidness to it. Her eyes refuse to look at him.

"What is it?"

"This vampire. Marie. She is dangerous." The words are soft, almost a whisper.

"All vampires are dangerous. Even the young ones." He watches the girl's face. Stone-like.

"This one is worse. We have tried to kill it before. Other hunters. Our hunters. Some I knew. All failed." A hint of emotion.

She is trying to hold it together. Keep the emotion in check.

"Alright. They didn't tell you where it is?"

"No."

"That seems odd."

"They never found out. She found them before they could find her location. Killed them as they searched for her."

"I see. What does she have on you? On your organization?"

"A list of our houses. Where we operate."

"And what does she want?"

"Money. More than we could give."

"So you need to get rid of her. And you need me to do it."

"Yes."

"All you have is in that dossier." Jack's head nods to the dark brown folder sitting on the desk beside the coffee service.

"Yes."

"Not much to go on."

"No."

"I might be able to help. I have a contact. He might tell us where this vampire is."

"You do?" Hope flirts with the girl's face.

"Yes. I'll set up a meeting."

"First we need to go to the armory."

Abby steps into the hall, turning to look at Jack. His boots move from wood to tile, the click hardening. Her lips straight, eyes clear. The sound of the linen of her slacks swish with each step.

She's wearing flats. His eyes notice as they take in her chosen attire. Her path through the maze is clear, a sign of her life in this house. It's a different path than the way in, leading to the armory, or so Jack hopes. Another turn and a heavy wood door ends the hall. The dim light of the place adding to the confusion of the maze.

A brightness that blinds and pains the eyes as the nob is turned and the door is opened. Jack's eyes adjust to the sunlight. Green upon green greets him. The smell of earth, grass, and livestock.

The smell of a farm. His thoughts focus on his surroundings, all his senses at work.

Abby steps onto the light stone path. Grass surrounds them. A line of trees on either side of the grass. He takes in the garden on one side, the cattle and horses on the other. Buzzing of bees. The slow movement of the livestock. The wind gently flowing between leaves. Pleasant.

"So, it's a working farm." The gravel in Jack's voice brings the girl's head around to face him.

"Yes. We grow our own food in the garden. Raise cattle. Pigs and chickens are further back. The smell can be overwhelming this time of year." Her pace quickens. A red barn looms ahead of them, and this is where she is leading him.

"I bet."

Abby steps through the open doors, shadows moving over her pixie frame to replace the bright sun. Jack follows, taking in the farm equipment. She moves through a stall. A calf looks up with lazy eyes, then returns to the fodder at its hooves. Her fingers push on a panel, a click, and it pops open. A small keypad, hidden behind, glows a faint green. Thin fingers move too quickly for Jack to catch the code. A pop and a pair of doors are revealed behind the panels beside the keypad.

"This way." Soft light glows from the top of the

elevator. She steps inside, turns, and faces Jack as he follows. The doors close silently. Jack's body lifts, gravity losing its power for a moment, then returns. His eyes watch the door.

"You have lots of secrets." He can feel her shift. He keeps his eyes forward.

"Yes. It is necessary."

"I'm sure it is." The push of extra gravity. The car stops. The doors open to a long room, lit from above by harsh bulbs. A man walks toward them. Crew-cut, good build, warm smile. His bronze hand juts toward the hunter. Jack takes it. The handshake is firm but friendly. No masculine gesturing here.

"It's a pleasure to meet you, Mr. Simpson. I've heard that you would be working with us and I selected a few items that I thought you would find useful." The crew-cut motions for Jack to follow. The black tee and light green slacks remind Jack of the military.

"You ex-military?"

"Yes. I was in the infantry for the first part. Fought in the desert. Then an armorer."

"Why the change?"

"Got tired of being shot at." The ex-soldier chuckles. "Names Sal. I run the armory for these folks. Nice enough gig. Food is good and they let me do my thing without too much poking around."

"Good to know."

"You military?" The smile on Sal's face peers at Jack as he leans against a waist-high table. Jack scans the daggers laid out before him. A short sword sits at the back.

"No. Never served." Jack's finger glides across the

dagger in front of him. So like the one in his own little armory back in San Diego.

"I figured you'd like that one. Heard you had something like that back home."

"Yeah."

"Anyway. You can check it out and if something happens, just let me know. Silver ain't cheap and the brass likes to keep tabs on this stuff."

"Sure." Jack takes the blade, slips it into his boot. Looks at Abby strapping a dirk to her ankle. He stands. Looks at Sal. The man grins.

I like this guy. Jack smiles inside.

"Heard you are going to be teaching Abby here how to do some hunting."

"Yeah."

"Better than the library, eh Abby?" Jack's eyes swing to the girl. Her face fixed.

"Yes. We should be going, Sal." Tension in the girl's voice. Sal seems not to notice.

"Sure. But don't be afraid to visit. It can get lonely down here." The sound of defeat in the armorer's voice tells Jack that this is true. The pair move past the blank walls, into the elevator. Jack turns as the doors close. Sal is putting the remaining blades in a cabinet below the tabletop. There's a sadness to his movements. Loneliness.

"Librarian?" The words come out as an accusation.

"Clerk, to be precise. I am the assistant master of the archives here."

No emotion. She's not happy to be found out.

"Do you have any training on hunting?" A cocked eye of displeasure glares at the pixie beside him.

"Only texts. I am physically capable. Strength and agility training. All members are required to be physically fit."

"But practical?"

"No. That is why I am working with you. My aunt thought it best."

"Did she?"

"Yes."

"I want to be clear. You need to listen to me. Hunting is not something that can be taught in a book. Believe me. It is a lesson I learned years ago. I need you to do as I say. Follow my lead. Even if it goes against your books. Can you do that?" The words soften. *This isn't what she wants. She's being forced into this. Just like me.*

"I will."

"Good. Then I think we will work well together."

"Thank you." Abby looks at him. The first break of the hard exterior showing through. He can tell that this means something to her, he is just not sure what that is.

❋ ❋ ❋

Sunlight blinds Jack as he steps out of the barn. Chirping birds, the lull of a cow in the distance. The humid earth, dampness has turned the gravel a darker color. The girl beside him looks at the house, her head turns slowly toward Jack. He watches her movement with cautious eyes.

"Your lead. Is it possible to meet today? This contact you think will get us Marie." The silvery voice asks in a flattened tone that is a contradiction. Abby's cocked eye waits for the answer. Silent. Demanding.

"Possible. I would have to call. Find out if he's still

alive." His eyes look out on the cattle moving through the wet grass, grazing with the lack of care only a domestic animal can have.

"Your contact may be dead?"

Is that surprise in her voice.

"Maybe. I'll call. But I'll need my phone. That's something you forgot to return to me." His turn to cock an eye. She looks away, toward the garden, away from piercing eyes.

"I will retrieve it. It is…"

The cool is breaking. She doesn't want to lie.

"Doesn't matter. I need the contacts to get my man. Otherwise, this is going to take a lot longer."

"Very well." Abby breathes deeply, letting the humidity fill her lungs, letting it calm her. "This way."

The crunch of gravel and Jack follows. She stops at the heavy door, looks at him.

She wants to say something.

"Out with it."

"What do you mean?"

"Don't be shy, there's a question on your mind and if I'm to train you, you'll need to not hold back. So, what's on your mind?"

"Do you think we can find this vampire?" Her voice softens with sadness. Jack studies the youthful eyes. Light brown, pretty in a childish way. Her head turns as her face reddens.

"Yes. What is it to you? Not a simple hunt. There's more to it than that." His hand touches her shoulder, lightly, with compassion. She remains motionless. Turns to him. A forced smile on her lips. Pain on her face.

"Another time. Now we must work to find this vampire." Her delicate hand pushes on the latch, the door swings into the sunlight. Gloom before them. They step into it. The sun disappearing with a click behind them. Her steps hurry them through the maze, to a door that is like all the others. A rap on the wood and a mumble within.

"I said come in." A faint voice from within. Abby turns the nob, swings the door into the room. Steps into the sun-washed chamber. A twin bed sits in a corner. A desk under the window, the thin man from the night before turns to look at the hunter and his helper.

"Jerry, this is Jack Simpson. He is the hunter that is to help us find Marie." Her voice softens. A kindness not heard in her words before.

"Yes. We have met, though briefly."

"Jack, this is my mentor."

"Not any longer." The thin man's words laced with venom as his eyes bare down on the man standing next to Abby.

"Yes, that is true, I have been transferred."

"Yes." Jerry hisses.

"We have come for Jack's phone. He requires it for a contact."

"It's over there. On the table. Take it. It is useless anyway. Typical rabble, nothing more." Jerry grunts.

His eyes return to the tomb in front of him. Abby moves slowly. Jack can see the sadness in her, the hurt. She takes Jack's phone. Looks at the man that had trained her, that is now ignoring her, and moves out of the room. Her steps take her toward the front of the house, at least that is Jack's best guess. He looks at the man's back. The movement of grief. Closes the door and follows his new assistant.

"Should I change before we see your contact?" Her voice is light, inquisitive.

"Yeah. Jeans and a tee would be best. He has a thing about people from money. Not sure what it is, but it's there." Jack's shoulders lift slightly toward his ears.

"I see." She stops, turns, looks the hunter in the eye. "Is that what you think? That I come from money?" Her head tilts slightly, questioning washing over her youthful face.

"It doesn't matter." The growl removes the look from Abby's face. She nods, turns, and moves forward. He follows. "I should reach out to him. Before we leave."

"The front porch is through those doors." The softness of her words eases him as the sunlight bellows through the floor-to-ceiling windows. Warm air flows through the open french doors. "I will be down in a moment." He watches as her light step takes her up the stairwell. Her pixie frame disappearing above him. Jack steps into the breeze, breathing in the early summer air, laced with the scent of fruit trees that dot the pasture.

"This place is nice." A smile creeps across his face, despite himself.

It disappears just as quickly as the cell phone is pulled from his pocket. A scan of the contacts. A finger pressed on the screen. The sound of dialing.

"What do you want?" The high thin voice, laced with pain, accuses the speaker.

"I need some information. Can we meet?"

"Don't have anything on your Tristen."

"Not him. A Marie. Local, causing some trouble. Blackmailing someone that I need info from. If I take care of her, then…"

"Then you get Tristen. Alright. You have anything but a name?"

"Like I said. Local. I assume that means within the state or one of the border states. Old from what I got."

"Ok. I'll look into it. Meet me at the dinner at five. Alone."

"I have someone working with me. She'll be coming along. Not an option to leave her behind."

"Fine. But no one else."

"Alright." Jack's finger-ends the call. He looks out at the cattle grazing. Waits for Abby to speak.

"So we are meeting today."

"Yes. Can you get us a car? I can drive."

"Sure." Jack watches her move away from him.

The light steps making her smaller in his eyes. He turns back to the cattle. The fruit trees. Finds an allure in them. Then blocks it out.

Chapter 10
Jeff

THE STENCH OF BROOKLYN ASSAULTS JACK AS HE STEPS OUT of the black town car. Abby is clad in faded jeans, tennis shoes, and a tight tee. Jack shakes his head slightly as his work boot grinds broken glass into the concrete. He stretches, leans in. The driver, another youth, looks back at him with the uneasy smile of uncertainty.

"Park it somewhere, not close. She'll call you when we're done." He stands, takes in the questioning look on the girl's face. "I told you Jeff doesn't trust money."

"I understand." The words do not match the tone. *She's not sure.*

He turns, looks at the dinner. The chrome trim with flecks of rust. The neon sign, blinking in the daylight, losing the nocturnal charm. His thoughts shift to the times before, when he was younger. The caress of soft fingers on bare skin brings him back before he can tumble down the nostalgia hole.

"We should get inside." The growl is a reaction. Again

her eyes question him, then lets it go. His hand pulls the chrome handle towards him. He waits. The girl enters.

"Thank you." There's true appreciation in those words. He steps into the cool air-conditioned room. Saliva pools under his tongue as the smell of diner cooking hits his nostrils. His eyes move across the open dining room by instinct. Worn tables, the laminate faded by years of cleaning. Vinyl booths, patched over and over. Bright lighting, showing all the flaws. The row of backless stools, bolted to the black and white checkered floor, separates the counter from the customer. A man in cook's whites works the grill. The slight smile showing a rare love of one's work.

"Anywhere you like." The smoker's growl comes from the weathered smile of the equally weathered woman. The waitress's uniform bulging around her large form.

"In the back?" The pleasantness of Jack's words causes the girl to look at him. Wonder in her eyes.

"Sure thing. We have a special going. Ham and eggs. Jim makes the best damn hash browns in town."

"We have another person coming. I think we'll wait until he gets here before ordering." Jack smiles at the large woman as he slides across the fake leather, settling in the middle of the seat. "But I would like some coffee, please. Black."

"And for you miss?" A wide smile beams down at the pair of hunters.

"Tea, with lemon and honey." The smile disappears at the dry response. The sound of shuffling fabric as the waitress scurries away.

"That was a bit hard." Jack leans back in the well-used booth.

"Hard?"

"Yeah. The off-handed way you ordered. Like she's a servant."

"She is our waitress."

"That doesn't mean you should be rude."

"I was not rude."

"But you were. You came off entitled. Arrogant. Not the best way to get what you want. Work on that. There's a time to be an asshole and a time to not be. Most of the time it is the time to not be." Jack's cocked head tells her it should be taken to heart. She nods, the lesson sinking in.

"I understand. I am not good with people. They are hard for me to understand."

"I can see that. You tend to turn a good time bad."

"I don't understand."

"Like with the waitress. She was being friendly. You treated her like a vending machine. A please or thank you goes a long way. So does a smile. In our line of work, it can come in handy. Hell, it can save your life."

"How so?" An eyebrow turns up curiously.

"Say we are looking for a vampire. Like we are now. She could have information on this Marie. Say we overhear something, get an idea that the waitress knows something. She's more likely to tell us if we've been nice. Human nature. Also, it's the right way to be with people."

"I see. And this Jeff?" Abby looks away, staring out the window onto the busy street.

She's tired of the lecture. Can't blame her.

"He's… complicated." Her pale brown eyes return to Jack's.

"Meaning?"

"He has issues."

"How did you meet?"

"I saved his life."

"How? A vampire?"

"No. It was a werewolf. He was a cop at the time. Patrolman here in New York."

"I didn't think werewolves lived in the city."

"This one must have strayed in."

"How did you save him?"

"You want to hear all this?"

"Yes."

"Alright. It was late. I was hunting down a lead on a young vampire that might have had info on Tristen. The streets were as empty as they ever get in the city. It was quiet. Not the nightlife part of town, more residential and shops. Anyway, it was pretty deserted. I heard something. At first, I didn't think anything of it. Maybe a fight or a couple had snuck off to fool around. The sounds weren't too distinct. As I got closer I could hear the moans. The whispered pleas. Then the soft growls. I thought it was a dog by the sound of it. But when I turned the corner. Looked down the alley. It was dark, but a werewolf is pretty distinctive. Anyway, it didn't notice me."

"I thought their senses are heightened?"

"They are, but it had prey. A dead cop and Jeff mangled. It was ready to feed. It's focus on the dead man. I moved in behind and slipped my blade into the back of its skull. The thing dropped."

"It was dead?"

"Yeah. Werewolves are easier to kill than vampires. Kill them like humans, only you need silver weapons. I'm a vampire hunter, so I always have one on me. And you should too, now that you are going down that route."

"So what happened?"

"The thing turned into its human form. Nude. Laying there in the filth. There was nothing to do for the dead cop. He was mangled. Face ripped up. I remember thinking that I felt bad for his family. Then the moans got my attention. Jeff, well I didn't know him then. He was trying to crawl away from the dead former werewolf. I stepped over the werewolf and tried to help him. He was pretty out of it. I saw the patrol car on the other end of the alley, that was what he was trying to get to. Anyway, I called it in on his radio. The dispatcher sent more cops and I gave a statement that I saw a group of large dogs run off when I came around the corner. I don't think they believed me, but they didn't push it. Jeff was taken to the hospital. I went to see him. His wife was there. It was hard for her, seeing him like that. Anyway, he never saw me. I only went once, and then moved on."

"How did he become a contact then?"

"He came to me. A couple of weeks later he tracked me down. I was in a little hotel by the water. We talked. He was grateful. I told him what happened. I could see it was a relief, he had seen the thing kill his partner and knew it was no pack of wild dogs. So, I told him about my search and he promised to help me."

"And now?"

"Now. Now he's bitter."

"Because of the attack?"

"Because he lost everything. His wife left him about a year after. His kids want nothing to do with him. He can't work and the pension he gets isn't much."

"That's unfortunate."

"It's hard. For a guy that was always the breadwinner. To become useless, at least in his own eyes, is a blow that pushed him over the edge. Anyway, that's him coming in the door. We can pick up on this later if you want."

"Sure."

She twists to look at the shattered form of a man hobbling toward them, the black hands turning pale as it griped the wooden cane. The scowl reads hate in the man's brown eyes. He stops, looks at the girl.

"You're in my spot." The rasp of a sound wheezes from the scared throat.

Abby slips out from the table and slides in beside Jack. The pain screams silently from the man's mangled face as he wills himself into the vinyl seat. His raspy breath reeks of alcohol.

"So what the fuck do you want this time, Jack?" Jeff growls.

Jack can see the look of shock creep into Abby's face as she watches Jeff's anger flow out of him. Jack's hand slips under the table and squeezes her knee. He can see her holding back whatever it was she was going to say.

"So nice to see you too, Jeff." The words whisper to the man across from him, calming him.

"Yeah."

"You look strung out. Using again?" The concern is subtle, but there.

"No. Not for a bit. Drinking mostly. Cheaper than smack. But I doubt you're here for an intervention." The scarred scowl is menacing, but nothing more than a bluff. "You want information on…"

Jeff looks up at the plump form sitting two coffees and a cup of tea on the worn table. He eyes the woman. Taking her in. His eyes follow her cheerful stride as it takes her into the kitchen.

"You were saying?" Jack's words bring the mess of a man back to the conversation.

"Yeah. Information. I found something on your vampire. If it's the same one you are looking for. Old one. Few hundred years old at least. So, she's not easy to find. In fact, I couldn't get anything on her. No location, town, nothing. Wherever she is, she's keeping it a secret."

"So it's a bust." Jack leans back, shoulders dropping. The sorrow in his voice raises an eyebrow on the scarred face across from him.

"Not exactly. She has a fledgling wandering around. I got info on her. Punk rock girl, or well vampire."

Jeff pulls a worn folder from his bag, slips it across the table. Jack looks at it. Opening it reveals a youth with green hair. A thin form. She's moving into a club. Seedy. Perfect for a vampire.

"This her?" Jack's eyes take in the vampire in the photo, letting the image burn into his memory.

"Yeah. Likes runaways. That's the club they go to. Well one of them anyway. She'll be there tonight. My informant tells me she hasn't fed in a couple of days. Scared of something. So you should have your chance to get whatever it is you need out of her."

"Thanks, Jeff." Jack slips the folder across the table, it disappears into the bag.

"I need to get going. Need to get in before it gets dark. These bastards know about me. At least I think they do. So, being out past sunset isn't a good idea." Jeff's grimace screams of pain as his addled body lifts itself from the seat.

"Alright." Jack can see the wet forming in the corner of the man's eyes. He can see the never-ending torment of suffering that the werewolf attack has lumped upon him.

"Be careful out there, Jack. These things are beginning to fear you."

"So I've heard."

"Then hear this. That's when animals, people, or monsters get really dangerous. When they feel trapped or in danger. You're not a two-bit hunter anymore. I'm hearing things about the crap you've done down in California out here. Watch your ass."

"I will." The shuffling sound of the man Jack saved so many years ago ends as he steps out into the protective sunlight. A light that is beginning to fade.

"What now?" The softness of Abby's voice is a hard shock compared to the sounds coming out of Jeff. Jack sips his coffee, letting heat slide down his throat.

"We find this vampire and then get Marie."

Chapter 11
Lily

"I DON'T THINK I'VE BEEN HERE BEFORE." NERVOUSNESS slips past the normally cool tone of Abby's words.

Her eyes dart. Bums gather themselves in a nest of cardboard, ragged blankets, and discarded clothing. Cheap wine, and for those lucky enough, cheaper liquor takes the worries of life away for a few brief hours. Urine, sour alcohol, and other unpleasantries assault the pair's nostrils. Pealing tatters of former posters, the bands having long performed their musical numbers, hang loosely from the concrete, brick, or glass that separates the hunters from the black voids beyond. Inky gloom is broken by the few working street lights, most of the street is in shadow.

Jack's eyes pierce the blackness, using his nose and ears to gauge the world around him. Abby looks at the furrowed brow, eyes scanning the alleyways. The line, short and moving quickly into the void left open by the steel cage and door lay ahead of them. Nothing marks the club's name. A blank wall greets the visitors. A place that is known by word of mouth, not a flashing sign inviting in anyone. A monster of a man towers over the patrons in their Doc Martins, skinny jeans, and red suspenders. Punk rock bands get free ad time from the youth's shirts.

"This is it." Jack mumbles just clearly enough for Abby to understand.

The hunters step behind the mohawk and his girl. Spikes on her collar almost as wide as her shoulders. She turns, looks at Abby. The sneer of being around one that is less than creeps over her young pale face. The girl's eyes drift to Jack, the expression slips away as the four uneven bars are comprehended.

"Rollin's rules." The squeak of a voice announces with unabashed pride. Jack's smile is hard, uncaring. The girl's eyes move away, a slight reddening of her cheeks and she moves to the bouncer. He nods her and the mohawk in.

"ID girl." The growl is just on the friendly side, but the eyes tighten on Jack. "Not looking for trouble tonight are you boy-o?"

"No."

"Then pay at the counter and keep the bottles unbroken."

"Sure thing."

The bouncer's eyes stay on Jack as he moves into the darkness of the club's entry. The sound of the man's voice growling out commands to the kid that follows Jack comes to his ears as he slips a pair of twenties to the skinhead inside the cage. Hands are stamped and the hunters move around a corner into the dim light of the bar.

"Is this what most clubs are like?" Abby, her eyes

absorbing the cheap high tops. The small bar serving beer only. Concrete, painted some dark color, black walls.

"No, it's a bit too Goth for a regular club. Most of them are a bit more flashy and inviting. They also serve more than beer. This is what you would call a dump, lower than a dive but higher up than a rave."

"Oh." The lack of understanding can just be heard in her reply. Jack nods her toward a hightop at the back of the room. Leans against it and takes in each patron, one at a time.

"I don't see the fledgling. I'll get us beers. Anything special?"

"Doesn't matter, I won't drink it anyway. I do not drink alcohol."

"Then I'll see if they have a soda or something, you need to look like you want to be here."

"Anything diet."

"Alright." Jack looks back to see the girl watching the door out of the corner of her eye.

Good. She's not being obvious.

Jack steps behind a blue-haired kid and his green-haired buddy. Both order beer, two kinds of domestic is all that is available. As his beer and Abby's soda slides across the makeshift bar top, Jack sees his prey. He tosses a twenty on the table, grabs the drinks, and shifts through the crowd of punk rock kids.

"I think that's her." Abby sips her diet soda as her eyes stay locked on the young vampire across the room.

"Yep. That's her." Jack leaves the beer untouched.

He watches as the vampire weaves her thin form through the gathering mass of human bodies. She disappears behind the larger party-goers, then back in view. Jack scans the people, taking in the loners in the crowd. He spots five distinct people. All of them by themselves. All of them look like street kids. Lights dim as the trio of lanky men step up to their instruments. The wall of fast and hard music assaults the ears. A grin forms on the hunter's lips. *I like these guys.*

A glance at Abby, her face twisted in a scowl of distaste that gives him a chuckle inside. Then back to the vampire. Her eyes fixed on a purple-haired girl. Jack watches her. She stands alone. The round high top devoid of any other person. There is excitement there as she takes in the sounds from the front of the room. Her body moves up and down to the beat of the bass. Her plaid print pants, sneakers, and crop top tee blend in with the rest of the crowd.

Jack's eyes move back to the vampire. Her frame lounging against the black wall, eyes intent on the girl. A slight grin. The teeth. Fangs. Just a glimmer. Enough to confirm his suspicions.

"It's her." He yells just loud enough for Abby to hear.

"We need to be sure."

"Saw the fangs. That's a vampire."

"What now?"

"We wait." Jack sips the beer, slowly. *Don't need to get light-headed on this one.*

He keeps his eyes on the vampire. It slips in and out of the crowd. Stalking the girl at the front of the room. Outside of the bright lights that the vampire would rather avoid. The desperation in the vampire is clear to the hunter. Her paleness is deeper than it should be. She needs to feed. Fear of something has kept her in the shadows. Thirst has brought her out. She moves closer to the purple-haired girl. Jack's eyes follow. The vampire slips beside her prey. A close-lipped grin, the girl's friendly smile. The pogo dance in front of them creating a cheap strobe light effect. The vampire leans in. The girl looks, a flicker of lust in her eyes. She says something, the vampire nods to the door. The girl shrugs, drains the beer on the table and joins the vampire as she moves to the exit.

"That didn't take long." Abby's voice struggles to get past the sound of punk rock.

"That vampire is starving. Really. I'll explain later, let's go." Jack moves through the crowd, Abby close behind. The line to get into the place has grown, but not by much and it gives little cover to the vampire and her prey as they walk past the colorful hairstyles.

The pair follow in the shadows. The vampire flirts, using her blossoming powers of persuasion. The girl looks at the vampire. Lust is there. She moves in. Kisses the vampire. Stops. Looks at her. Something is said. Jack strains to hear, but the pair are too far away. Any closer and it would be suspicious. Jack pulls Abby to him, moves close. The vampire looks back. Sees another couple on the deserted street. A flash of fangs is seen from the corner of Jack's eye. Abby struggles in his arms. He looks at her. Stern eyes bore into her.

"Play along. She's on to us. We need to be lovers out on a stroll." The whisper breaks the silence.

She nods. Moves against him, her head leaning against his chest. He uses the corner of his eye to watch the vampire and her prey move into the gloom of the night. His hands move Abby away from him. She looks down the sidewalk. The vampire and girl have become silhouettes in the inky night.

"Do we follow?" Abby whispers.

It is the same question Jack is asking himself. The vampire has seen them. Knows they are there. It's a chance that has to be made and the hunter knows it. He has to get Marie's location from the fledge. Then he can get Tristan.

"Yes." His arm slips behind her.

A hand drops onto her shoulder, as a lover would do. She looks at his. Eyes questioning. Mouth silent.

"Need to keep the illusion. Hunters work alone, normally. This will give us an edge. And an edge is always good when dealing with a vampire. Especially one that is as jittery as this one." Jack explains softly.

"That makes sense." She nods as she moves closer.

He can feel the awkwardness of it. The foreign sensation of being this close to him.

"You haven't been close to men much."

"My aunt forbids it."

"So you haven't dated."

"Most of the members of the Society are too old. The youth are in training and it is forbidden to date those in training." He can see the sadness in her eyes. Just there, just under the surface.

"It must be lonely."

"It is. I have grown accustomed to this life. Other than my mentor and my aunt, you are the only person I have spent much time with. I have led a sheltered life. Books and scrolls. Old tombs in a basement have been my only true companions. That is why I find it so odd

that my Aunt would assign me to you. To be a hunter."
Abby's eyes remain on the vampire's shadowy figure as she
whispers the words with a sadness Jack can understand.

"It will not get easier. Being a hunter. It is a lonely life.
Friends barely exist. Loved ones are a liability. You are
never safe. A vampire hunter is always in danger from the
things that they hunt. Intelligent monsters are the most
dangerous. And this one has found its home."

"I see." Abby says with tears being held back.

Both hunter's eyes follow the vampire and her prey
into the hotel. A sign, neon letters black from lack of
maintenance. The few steps leading up to the glass door
with a metal frame. A pair of bums, snuggled in an alcove,
sleep off the nights drunk. The hunters move up the
stairs, two at a time. The vampire and her prey take the
first steps up to the second floor. Jack and Abby move in.
A stench of mildew hits their nostrils. Darkness blankets
the lobby. No watchman. The tile, clean but stained with
years of use under their feet. Wood steps, the familiar
worn curve in the middle. They take this in silence, two
at a time. Stopping before the gloom of the hall. Jack peers
around the corner. The vampire is entering a room. Her
head swivels. Searching for prying eyes. Seeing none, she
slips inside. Jack turns to Abby. She looks at him. Eyes
full of questions.

"We give it a few minutes. I have the room. We go
in. Get what we need and get out. This is not going to be
pretty. Torture most likely. Can you handle that?" Jack's
words come out fast and just loud enough for Abby to
hear him.

"I will do what I must." The stern tone tells Jack that she will. That her strength is more than he expected.

He nods. Takes a breath and moves into the hall. Their feet tap softly on the worn carpet. They get to the door. Try the handle. It turns.

In her lust to feed, the damn thing forgot to lock the door. A grin on his face as the door swings slowly open.

Chapter 12
Tabitha

JACK'S EYES FOCUS ON THE VAMPIRE IN FRONT OF HIM, THE mouth moving across the neck. Purple hair pushed aside, exposing the smooth white flesh. Fangs slipping into the open. The vampire's head tilts back. Eyes closed as she waits for the taste of fresh blood. The victim coos as pale fingers gently pinch the nipple under her t-shirt.

Jack charges. The crunch of a breaking arm sends a howl out of the vampire as his shoulder slams heavily into the creature. The momentum sends her thin form smashing into the wall. Her head smashes into the plaster. Eyes flutter. Close. The creature's body crumples to the mildewed carpet, leaving a hole in the plaster where the head once was. Screams turn Jack to the girl. He grabs the vampire, pulling it off the floor. Abby hand covers the girl's mouth. Her eyes role with the terror of what is happening to and around her. Her new lover, battered and being dragged toward the bed that she was looking so forward to being loved in.

"Hush. This thing was going to kill you. We saved your life. Now sit and be silent." Abby growls.

The stern tone surprises Jack. An eyebrow raises as he realizes this is a side of his apprentice that has not shown itself before. The stern librarian. A flicker of a smile flashes across his lips.

The girl with the purple hair flops onto a wooden chair. Tears form in her eyes as they bounce from Abby to Jack. Her mind unable to comprehend what is happening. They settle on Jack as he pulls the sheets from the bed.

The vampire's body is tossed on the empty mattress. It bounces twice, then lays motionless on the stained and bare mattress. Ripping of linens mixes with the click of the closing door and the girl's fear holds her in place as the strips of torn cloth drop to the mattress from the man's strong hands. A small bottle is pulled from his pocket, the women watch it open. The scent of garlic takes the room. Light oil drips down on the cloth as Jack's large hands toss the strips, ensuring they are fully coated.

"Tie her up." Jack's grunt pulls Abby into action. She grabs a strip of the sheet, moves to the girl, and binds her to the chair.

"What are you going to do to me?" The tremor of fear matches the look in the girl's eyes. Her mind finally returning from the frozen shock that has gripped it.

"Nothing." The sound of Abby's voice has lightened.

The strip of cloth slips between the girl's lips, teeth bite into it. Abby turns to watch Jack finish tying the vampire to the bed. The girl's eyes, wide with fear, move from one hunter to the other. Then to the new found lover bound to the bed.

"She won't be out long. Get your people on the phone. Have a car ready to pick us up. This won't take long. And you." Jack's focus moves the victim, her body limp in the chair. "You need to be a little more careful who you wander off with. This thing would have drained you. Dumped your body in an alley. Then went out to find another trusting young soul to feed on. It's a vampire. I can see your eyes. You think I'm lying. I'm not. You'll see when the sun comes up. That thing you thought was a cute girl. A lover for the night. It'll be dust in an hour."

All eyes move to the vampire. Her body spread eagle on the mattress. Eyes open slowly. Confusion. Struggle. Anger.

"What the fuck do you think you are doing? Do you know what the fuck I am? I'll drain you of your fucking life's blood." Hate drips from the threats. Narrow eyes pierce the man's frame as he moves closer, bending. Jack looks at the creature. No emotion.

"No, you won't." The vampire's face twists in fear as the low growl reaches her ears.

"You can't do this." The hard tone softens, the fear cutting through the bitter hate.

Jack's face remains cold, hard. His eyes take in the vampire. Her body pulls against the linen binding her to the bed frame. Her eyes return to hate, the momentary fear drifting away.

"You fucking scum." The whisper hisses past the enlarged canines.

Her eyes narrow. Jack stands, letting the vampire fail to break free of the strips of bedding. Garlic weakening the creature. His head turns to Abby, watching in silence.

She's taking notes. Observing the process.

His eyes move to the purple-haired victim bound to the chair. Gagged. Eyes wide with fear, wet forming at the corners.

"Check for bites. This thing might have gotten to her before we got in the room." The calm of his voice brings all eyes to him. They look at him, quiet, uncertain. "Do it. Now." His tone deepens.

Abby moves, pushing hair from the girl's neck. Examining the neck, shoulders, arms. She pulls down the girls shirt, exams her breasts and find them free of the vampires touch. Jack turns to the bound vampire. He is met with the glare of hate.

"I am going to ask you some questions. You are going to answer them." The calm in his voice is almost soothing, pleasant.

Still, the vampire's eyes narrow as she watches him pull the blade from his boot. Silver flashes before the vampire's eyes. A glimmer of fear again flits past and disappears.

"And if I don't?" The hiss of hate slips past the undead lips.

"Then you will feel pain like you have never felt before. Believe me when I say this to you. I have become quite good at inflicting pain. And this is a silver blade. You will not heal like you normally would. You will scar. Pain will stay with you for the rest of your undead life."

The blade moves to the girl's face. Caresses her cheek. Eyes widen as the fear returns to the vampire. Now it stays with the young vampire. The creature trembles as Jack caresses the monster with the edge of the blade.

"What do you want?" The tremble in the vampire's voice tells Jack he has her.

"I want to know where the one that made you is?" He sits on the edge of the bed, twisting to look the bound vampire in the eyes. His body against hers. The dagger moving slowly over her flesh. "Can you tell me that?"

"She would kill me." The terror causes a stammer in the vampire's words. Tears begin to creep into the edges of her eyes. "You don't understand how strong she is."

"I do. But I need to destroy her. And to do that you will need to tell me where she is." The tip of the blade indents the pale skin of the vampire's chest. Jack can see the burning sensation she must be feeling in the wince of her eyes.

"Your little bullshit isn't going to work on me." The pain in the vampire's eyes mix with the hate it beams at the man hovering over her bound body. Then Jack sees something else in those eyes, it is behind the hate. It is fear. Not of him, but of the one that made her.

"No bullshit here. Just want to know where Marie is. And I will kill her. You will not have to worry about her coming after you. Finding you. Torturing you. She will be gone. But I can see you need something to encourage you." The blade slips beneath the pale skin. Blood pools around the wound. The vampire's teeth bare as the pain screams out of her chest.

"You fuck!" She howls, tears dripping slowly down the side of her face. "You can torture me all you want. I can't give that bitch up. I fucking can't"

"Yeah, but you will. And the pain, well, it's going to get much worse. That mark. It's going to stay with you until you die. I can keep going. Have you seen some of your kind out there? The ones missing fingers? That was me. Now, I think I can move to a pinky if you're not ready to talk."

Jack's hand moves slowly, the wide eyes of the vampire on it, toward the bound hand. The realization of who she is dealing with comes to her. Fear washes over the vampire. It's eyes look at the hunter in front of her and knows. Knows that it is doomed.

"No. No. I'll tell you what you want. I've seen them. the disfigured. I can't go on like that. She's…" A sweat breaks through the pale flesh. Wide eyes. She bites her lip.

"Yes?" The blade touches the small finger. Her eyes flicker to the blade, then back to the man's solemn expression.

"She's upstate. A little town named Jasper. Farmland. Smells like cow shit. I hated it. I have no love of that bitch. But. Well. She's powerful. Suppose to be an ancient or some shit like that. I don't know. I didn't play by her mad rules. Sleeping in a crypt on stone. Fuck that. I want a soft bed. But that's where she is. Now, you can let me go right?"

The pleading eyes hide the danger that is behind them. Jack watches the vampire twist her arm, trying to free herself. The garlic doing it's job. The eyes widen as his smile looks down at her.

"I never said anything about letting you go back out there and kill."

The dagger slips into his boot. He stands. The vampire looks at him. Her mouth moves but nothing comes out. His fingers grip the string beside the window. He pulls down, the blinds slide up. Orange brightens the dawn sky. Her eyes widen. Her lip quivers. Then the thrash of limbs straining against the cloth.

"Let me out, you bastard!" The scream is desperate, strained.

He steps away, letting the sunlight illuminate the wall opposite him. The vampire watches the light creep down the wall. Jack looks at the purple-haired girl. The gag in place. Eyebrows bunched together. The lack of understanding in the slightly cocked head.

"Sun will kill her. She'll be dust in a few minutes. Then you'll see what it is that you wanted to bed with. A monster. A real monster. Remember girl, they exist. And also remember. No matter who you tell, what you say, they will never believe you." He looks back at the vampire. Arms and legs straining against the restraints that bind her to the stripped bed.

"Please?" The tears in her eyes match the ones in her words. She looks to see the light just missing her hand and foot. The pleading eyes return to Jack. His face is hard, cold, uncaring.

The girl watches, Abby standing behind her, as the blistering skin bubbles on the sunlit hand. The vampire howls, the pain in her eyes drip onto the empty mattress. The bubbles move up the arm, to the chest. To the face. Past the body that is turning to char. The vampire's form, now a blackened mess, lays still. It crumbles. Breaks in the light. Grey dust is all that remains. Jack turns to the would-be victim.

"This is your lover. This is what she is." He moves past the girl.

She looks at him. Questions in her eyes. His head nods to the door. Abby moves to the girl's clothe strips.

"No. She can explain to the maid why she is tied to a chair."

Jack steps out into the hall, Abby behind him. He looks in to see the girl looking at the pile of dust. The remains of the woman that whispered sweet nothings past the purple-hair. The girl disappears from view as the door clicks shut. Jack walks away from the room, Abby beside him.

"What do we do now?" Abby's whisper just heard over the creek of the steps the pair walk down. Sunlight, slipping through the dirty windows that still hold glass, lights the lobby that is in front of them.

"We go up north. Find this town, Jasper is what she called it." Jack's shoulders move slightly up as his boot touches the lobby floor. "Then we find out where in Jasper This Marie is at. Tell me. What do we have so far?"

"She's in Jasper, unless the vampire lied."

Cool morning air hits them as the step out of the hotel lobby. The lack mildew stench, fills the hunters nostrils. Jack takes it in, breathing deep. Letting the stench of the hotel leave his lungs.

"Correct. But assuming the vampire was telling the truth. What then?" Jack watches the girl slip into the back of the black sedan. The youth standing at attention, eyes focused away from them.

"You don't have to be so formal with me. I'm not that important." The boy's eyes jump to the hunter. His smile easing the boy. Jack watches the shoulders drop, the knuckles regain color.

"Thank you, sir." The slight stutter makes the corner of the hunter mouth grow.

"Call me Jack. Everyone else does." The hard hand pats the suited shoulder. Jack nods as he takes his place beside the girl watching the interaction.

"What was that about?" Unsure eyes try to read him.

"Being friendly. Your group. Well, you guys take yourselves to seriously. We all are trying to do a job. Might as well have some fun with it. Anyway, I thought he was going to pass out, standing there like that."

"I see. You are trying to build camaraderie."

"Something like that. But you are moving away from your lesson. What are we going to do when we get to Jasper?" His cocked eye grills the girl.

"We will search out the area for the vampire."

"How?"

"Ask questions of the locals. Look for anything suspicious."

"That could get back to her, to Marie."

"Yes, but I don't see another option. We need information."

"There are other ways to get information. Look up the area on the net. Marie is on a farm. At least that is what our deceased vampire told us. Also, it is somewhat secluded. Those are two clues we can use to narrow down the search. And no one will know we are looking. A vampire like Marie has to have connections. People in the local government. Cops, politicians. We need to bypass them. Get the information another way."

"I see. I hadn't thought of it that way."

"And that is why you need to listen and learn. You're

doing good so far, but you need to remember to stay focused. Stay on top of things. And most importantly, things go south fast. A vampire can throw all kinds of wrenches into the works. When they do, you have to think fast, because you're not going to overpower them. Physical confrontation should be avoided at all costs. They are stronger, more powerful. But their minds, unlike the myths, are not any better than ours. Though their memories are. Remember that and you'll live to see another day."

"I see. Thank you."

"Just listen." Jack's eyes return to the mansion growing closer to him.

"I will. Do we leave today?"

"No, tomorrow. I need to research and we need sleep. I need you to set up a car for us. Something middle class. We'll travel as a couple. Vacationing. That'll bring less suspicion. A trip away from the kids. You can book the hotel. I'll search for the most likely farms that Marie will be using." Jack steps out of the car, standing beside the chauffeur as Abby slides across the bench seat.

"I can do that. Anything else?" Abby asks, her hands pulling down her top. The driver moving away from the hunters.

"Get some sleep. We haven't been to bed since yesterday. Is my room still the same? Also, I need a computer with internet access."

"Your room will remain yours during your stay with us. I will have someone bring you a computer for your research. Anything else required?"

"No, I think that'll do." Jack's voice shows the lack of

sleep. He's tired, but there are things that need to be done before the dream of a soft bed can come true. "Yeah, one other thing. Coffee. Strong coffee." Her smile is all the answer he needs as the part ways. His path leading to the little room, hers to somewhere within the complex that is growing on him.

Chapter 13
Abby

JACK TURNS TO THE OAK DOOR THAT SEPARATES HIM FROM the hall. The rap of knuckles on wood resounds through the small room again. He lets it stand, clicking the little locks that hold the lid of the suitcase to its body. Another rap of flesh on wood.

"Come in." His voice is calm, pleasant. The sleep has done wonders for his mental state. *Twelve hours straight. I haven't slept like that since, well, before the attack I would say.*

"The car is ready. Have you finished packing?" The light voice is comforting.

He turns, bag in hand, to see Abby looking at him in that curious way that has become her go to when dealing with him. Her own suitcase in hand.

"Yeah. Let's get going. I'd like to get there and look into some of the farms I think might be Marie's lair." His steps are light on the hardwood, leaving little sound for the girl's ears to pick up.

"As requested, the car is something middle class." Her smile is thin, though genuine.

Her head turns to the hall in front of them. She leads the way to the main entrance of the manor. Jack watches her, scanning the outfit she has chosen, as a few of the lower level members of the Society slip past them. A few look at the girl. The faint shock in their expressions shows that is not something the she is known for wearing.

"That's something different." His head nodding to the mini-skirt and tee combination. Sandals complete the look. College girl chic.

"I was going for the younger woman married to the older man look." The raised eyebrow and impish smile hints at a sense of humor that Jack didn't realize the girl had.

"Yeah, I'm a bit older." His shrug is casual. It's followed by a chuckle as they slip into the mid-size sedan.

"It should take us a couple hours to get to Jasper, maybe less depending on traffic." Her tone returns to business. The look of something, not quiet fear, maybe caution, creeps into her eyes.

"Well, it'll give us time to get to know each other a little better. I'd like to hear your story." He says as the sound of the engine comes to life.

The car moves past the little gate and onto the country road. Abby stares silently out of the window. Jack looks at her. Sees the discomfort as something in her past bubbles up into her mind.

"But that can wait. I would like to go over what we have in store for us first." Her face lightens, a tinge of a smile is on her lips as she turns to him.

"We'll be staying at a little hotel in town. It has all we need. Internet and restaurants that are close."

"Is it close to the center of town?"

"Yes, why?"

"We'll need to hit the country recorder."

"Why?"

"Get the plans to the farmhouse. That's how we figure out which one it is. I can only do so much on the net. The rest will be good old fashioned leg work." He laughs at himself as she looks at him with a cocked eye.

"How will you get them to allow you to look at those plans."

"I'll pose as an architect."

"That is your training?"

"Yes."

"Do you use it often?"

"Sometimes. Makes it easier to figure out where the secret rooms are. If there is a void, an area that is just not making sense. That's going to be your vampire lair. Sometimes there's more than one, but normally it's just the one. Understanding layout makes that easier." Jack shrugs as the dairy farms fly past.

"Did you work in architecture?"

"Yeah. I did it for years. I ran a small firm. Had employees. Did housing mostly. I liked it. Worked with families to give them their dream homes. Mostly wealthy people, but people all the same."

"So you worked for the wealthy, those with means?"

"And the poor. I worked with organizations that provided housing to those that have very little. Did some military housing too."

"Did you enjoy it?"

"Yeah, I did. I would still be doing it if certain things hadn't happened the way they did. But that's for another time. What I'd like to know is how you got into this. A young girl doesn't seem to be a good match for that mansion your Aunt runs."

"No."

"So, how did you end up there?"

"My parents died. I was three. I really don't remember much about them. Sometimes I get little flashes. Mostly of my mother."

"How?"

"I don't know. It's a memory thing."

"No, how did they die?"

"It was a vampire. In Paris. Along the river. They went out for a walk. Vacation. The vampire found them walking along a dark path. It attacked my father first, then my mother. Drained them both."

"You don't seem very upset about it."

"I didn't really know them. I have been told that I cried for a week, then I just stopped. I don't remember being emotional. Some would say I am reserved. My mentor believes it has to do with loosing my parents at such a formative time in my life. I don't know if that is why, but I tend to not get emotional."

"I've noticed that. You have trouble with people. Reading them. Being able to relate."

"Yes."

"What happened after you moved in with your Aunt?"

"I was tutored. Some of the best minds belong to the Society. I was given an education that most would envy.

It was home schooling and I moved through my classes quickly. I graduated at sixteen. Went on to study in the archives and have been there ever since."

"Until now."

"Yes, until now."

"You seem to like the research. Why do this?"

"My Aunt. She feels that it is important that I learn all aspects of the Society. Even the dangerous ones."

"So that's where I come in. To teach you."

"That is what I would assume. My Aunt is not one to speak about her plans."

"I noticed that too."

"She is a private woman. She likes to keep things to herself. It is her way."

"And you?"

"You could say I am the same. I keep to myself. I prefer books to people. Knowledge is something that comforts me. I have read most of the archives contents over the years. All but the most secretive texts. Even those I have been through."

"And what have you learned?"

"That the creatures that we hunt can be monstrous. Yet, there is a beauty to this evil. Still it is evil none the less."

"Vampire lore. What do you know about that?"

"It's incomplete, fragmented. Too many conflicting legends. What we do know is that silver can hurt them. Wild rose and garlic weaken them. Fire will consume them. Sunlight is deadly. Removing the head is the only way to stop them."

"A stake will work too."

"I did not know that. It is in legend, but never confirmed by our researchers. Have you used this technique?"

"Yes. It works. Paralyzes them. They can see and hear but have no motor functions."

"Fascinating. I will have to add that to the archives."

"I'm surprised you didn't know that. Haven't your hunters told you about that trick?"

"I don't think it's common knowledge."

"Funny, I figured it would be."

"Here is the turn." Abby points as Jack pulls off the highway, into the hamlet with its tree lined main street. The hotel, its cottage style one story structure with well-manicured grounds spreads out on the outer edge of the downtown. A steeple peaks through the green canopy.

"Nice place."

"Yes, my aunt suggested it." Abby says as she stepped out of the car, moving to the trunk.

"Has she been here?" Jack placed the suitcase on the asphalt.

"I believe so. It might be why the vampire took an interest in our organization." She wheeled the larger bag behind her as Jack shut the truck and followed her under the hotel's awning. The larger suitcase in hand.

"That would make sense. Come on, let's get inside and get settled in. I want to get to the recorder's office before it closes." Jack opens the door, letting her walk in. Her smile has a warmth to it that he hasn't seen before.

"Yes, then we can find somewhere to eat." The clerk lifts his eyes from the puzzle before him as the sound of

Abby's voice drifts to his ears. The smile grows as they move closer.

"Sure." Jack leans against the counter as Abby faces the grey bearded grin.

"Checking in?"

"Yes, we have a reservation. For Simpson."

"Yes, a king. It's down the hall. There's a separate entrance that the key card will open. It leads to the parking lot. Closer to the room."

"Good to know." The smile in Jack's words give the older man a chuckle.

"You two here for a little quiet? It's about the only thing we got in this town."

"Away from the kids." The chuckle from Jack gets a knowing nod from the older man.

"I hear ya there. Mine are all grown up, but it was nice to get away for a bit with the misses. Now I wish they would come around more. Live down in the city now."

"Well we have a while before that'll be our problem." Jack smiles as the old man slides the keycard through a reader behind the counter.

"Use the card on file?"

"Yes, please." Abby's reply is short, the man grows quiet. Jack looks at her, the frown leering. "I'm sorry. It's been a long drive."

"And our youngest was up all night. Grandpa shouldn't have brought all the sweets with him." The clerk's shoulders loosen, the smile returns.

"I got ya there. Don't worry miss, I've had those days. But now it's my turn to bring the candy." His body shakes slightly as the chuckle leaves his thin frame. "I think you're all set. Room is down the hall and to the left. If you need anything, give me a call."

"Yeah, I do have a question for you." Jack asks with a smile.

"What's that?"

"Where's a good place to eat?"

"Depends on what you're looking for?"

"Something nice." Abby smiles, her tone softing.

"Oh, that would be Charley's. Best steaks around. A little pricey, but worth it if you are going for a nice dinner out."

"Thanks." Jack takes the key card.

"Tell 'em Mike sent you." The clerk gives a friendly wave as the pair move down the hall toward their room.

Chapter 19

Jasper

JACK LOOKS AT ABBY, HER HAIR PULLED BACK BEHIND HER ears. A tinge of a smile on her lips as the warm summer air teases the bottom of her sundress. The bold yellow with flecks of blue birds is pleasant to the eye. The shade of overhanging limbs keeps the heat of the sun off their bare skin. The scent of freshly mowed grass is in the air. The landscaper, a man in his thirties and what looks to be his daughter, pile trimmings into an old pick up truck beside the freshly mowed round about. A huge oak provides relief to the pair as they complete their task. Jack's eyes return to the girl beside him. She looks up, eyebrows furloughed with a slightly cocked head.

"Yes?" Abby's voice is high and pleasant. The smile remains, the but eyes question.

"Nothing. Just looking at this place. So quiet. It's nice." His shrug is an apology for something he hasn't done. More habit than need.

"Yes. It is pleasant. Picturesque really." Her nostrils

flair as the summer air is pulled into her lungs. "The air is like home. The smell of grass. The rustle of the leaves. It's comforting."

"Yeah, I guess it is. I was raised in the city. Well, suburbs. Not much of a country feel to it. But it is nice."

Her smile broadens. "I think that is the county recorder's office." Her head motions to the stone facade ahead of them. The grey stained by years of rain and snow. The lintel with 'county building' carved into the stone. Glass and aluminum doors fit neatly into the opening set three steps above the cobble stone walkway.

"Looks like we have a half hour to get what we need." Jack's eyes scan the sign in front of the door. "The recorder is on the first floor." He pulls the door open, Abby slides past him into the air conditioned coolness. The fluorescent lights providing the artificial glow that feels like bureaucracy.

"Do we just go in?" Abby asked.

"I called ahead. While you were in the shower." His hand turns the brass handle, pulls the door toward him, lets the girl step inside.

They are greeted by wooden chairs lined against the beige wall. A heavy wooden counter separates them from the youthful looking woman that watches them move toward her. Sunlight glows behind her from the ribbon windows that line the wall at the ceiling. She smiles with a clerks passion as Jack leans against the counter, his smile more genuine.

"How can I help you?" The boredom from the clerk gives Jack a chuckle. Her eyes look him over. The button down short sleeve shirt, light blue and fitting tight against his muscular chest. The jeans, loose and faded. The work boots. Her smile changes to something a little more real.

"I have an appointment."

"You must be Mr. Simpson. You wanted to look at some properties?" The girl reaches under the counter. "I've pulled the ones that you are interested in." She places three rolls on the counter in front of Jack.

"Good."

"Would you like some time to study them? You mentioned your client is in a hurry to select a site."

"Yes, that would be nice. Can I look at them here?" Jack flashes a smile at the girl. Her smile grows as he opens the first set of plans. The layout showing him that this is the house that the vampire is in. The compound like layout. The buildings for the humans that watch over the vampire during the day. The isolation, the use of a national forest on three sides to provide an additional buffer from the prying eyes of neighbors. Only the main road, set a half mile from the structures, is open to easy access to the house. He opens the other plans, glances. Can see they are not suitable for an ancient vampire's lair. They don't have the void.

"I think I have what I need for my client. Can I get a copy of this one. The isolation is just what he's looking for." Jack slides the plans toward the clerk.

"Sure. It's a nice place." Something in her tone catches Jack's attention. A nervousness.

"Have you been there?"

"Yeah. Couple years ago. Big party for Halloween. I was still in high school, a senior."

"Is it nice?"

"Yeah. Strange though."

"How?"

"The people. Weird. Most people stay away from it. A lot of rumors. Some say it's a cult that's out there. They grow their own food and make beer for the local restaurants."

"Well, you might not have to worry about that soon. It might be the perfect location for my client."

"That would be nice. Those people give me the creeps. Well, let me get you the copies. I'll be right back."

"Thanks." Jack and Abby watch the girl slip into the back. She looks at him.

"That was too easy." Abby whispers.

"Not really. It's how things are done. This was somewhat routine. I sent fake documents giving permission to look over the plans. That there might be a pending sell."

"I see." The pair look at the clerk as she returns to the lobby. A roll of plans in her hand.

"Here you go. That'll be twenty dollars." She smiles as she slides the plans toward Jack, the receipt taped to them.

"Here you go." He pulls a twenty out of his wallet and hands it to the girl.

"Thanks." The clerk smiles as she rings up the plans. Jack waves as he and Abby walk out of the lobby.

"Now, let's get some food." Jack smiles.

✳ ✳ ✳

The light is still bright as the pair of hunters move out into the little downtown of Jasper, New York. The landscaper and his daughter have disappeared, leaving a few of the townspeople to stroll along the circular sidewalk. The steakhouse, recommended by the hotel clerk, sits on the opposite side of the round about.

"I think that's the steak place. You want to check it out?" Jack asks as the smell of charred beef lingers through the air.

"Yes. I am famished." Abby shifts toward the restaurant, Jack beside her.

They move past the few shops that are open in silence, enjoying the picturesque view of small town New York. The town folk greet them with smiles and simple hellos, that the pair return. Soon, they slip out of the warmth of the summer air into the cool of the dark steak house interior. Wood paneled walls and flooring greet them. A light colored plaster ceiling, devoid of lighting that is placed on the walls increased the romantic ambiance that the designer has tried to convey. Jack appreciates the thought, but dislikes the result. He keeps this to himself as the girl in front takes them to their seats in the back of the main floor. This is done with little chit chat, which Jack finds odd, but he let's it go. The pair slide into the booth that seems to remind Jack of a Black Angus. He chuckles at the thought. This brings Abby's eyes to his.

"What is it?" The words are soft, whisper like.

"Oh, nothing. It's this place. It hit me. It reminds me of a Black Angus Steakhouse. The way the seating is separated to make it feel like you have your own little private spot. It just tickled me is all. But they do have a good selection on the menu."

"Yes, I think I'll get the fish. Trout has always been a

favorite of mine." Abby says as she places the menu on the table that separates the two hunters. "And you?"

"Ribeye for me. I love a good steak." He watches as the waiter, a young man, moves with a grace that suggested dance training. The man slides across the near empty room and stops at the edge of the hunter's table.

"Good evening. I am Sam and I will be taking care of you this evening. We do have a special, it is the salmon. It arrived this afternoon. What would you like to drink?" The words slip out of the youth with a slight lisp as his hand hovers over the plain white paper encased in black leather.

"White wine, please." Abby says softly.

"Sam Adams." Jack replies with a smile. "And I think we are ready to order."

"Very good. Miss?" The waiter scribbles down the drink orders as he waits.

"The salmon. It's fresh today?"

"Yes?"

"And the vegetable melody and rice."

"Sir?"

"The ribeye, medium. A baked potato, butter only. And the vegetable melody. Italian dressing on the salad."

"Very good. I will get that right in. I'll be right back with your drinks and some bread."

"Thank you." Jack adds as the waiter rushes off to get their order in. He looks at the girl across from him, her youth.

"What is it?" She asks as her eyes look up at him. "Do I have something on my dress?"

"No. I was just wondering. About this vampire of

ours. Marie. What kinds of defenses she is going to have. That estate of her's. It's good sized. I'm sure that there are going to be human guards and patrols. The cult thing is a common rouse for vampires. You know that some of the famous cult leaders have been vampires."

"I can believe that." The sound makes Abby jump and Jack look quickly to the edge of the table as the waiter sets down the drinks and bread.

"I apologize if I startled you. I just over heard you talking about cults. We have one here. Just north." The waiter smiles. "If that is something you are interested in, I can tell you a little bit about it. As you can see it's a slow night." He motions to the empty tables.

"That would be nice, if it won't get you in trouble." Jack says softly. The waiter rolls his eyes and chuckles in a feminine way.

"Tonight I think you'll be one of my only customers. Town's having a big spaghetti dinner for the fire brigade. Everyone is out there. Mayor, councilors and all the people that would normally come in here. Well almost everybody. You have the place to yourself." The waiter laugh's causally. He grabs a chair and slides it over to edge of the table. "Call it dinner and a story." The youth giggles as the hunters look at each other, not sure how to handle the chatting young man sitting between them.

"Ok, I'll bite." Jack says, his composure returning.

"I bet you do, you're a lucky one miss." He says with a wink thrown in Abby's direction.

"The cult?" Abby says politely.

"Oh, yeah. Well, they moved in a while back. Had a big bash. Halloween. I was home from school that weekend and went. Great party. But then it stopped. Got quiet. There was a group of them. All dressed in soldier outfits. Then others were dressed in really naughty outfits. Sexual. Some of the townsfolk didn't like that. I thought it was a bit tacky, but what the hell, it was Halloween and you should be a bit slutty on that holiday. What got me the most was the foursome. Two girls and two boys. Young looking all of them. One girl was in charge. She looked pretty young to be bossing everyone around, but that's what she did. Pale. All of them. Dressed as vampires. That's what made me think of it. When you said that cult leaders are like vampires."

"I see." Jack says with a smile as he lifts the beer to his lips.

"Anyway, they didn't eat or drink anything. I thought that was strange. I found a cute boy and we snuck off together. One of the cult boys. Well after we, you know…"

"Yes, I know." Jack says firmly. Hoping the waiter will skip the steamy details.

"Well, after, we started talking. Him more than me. I told him I was in school and such. But he just started gushing out how they moved from Florida and it is so cold here and the contractors, which he had to deal with, all came from Vermont, I think is was Vermont. So they had to get the place remodeled. I laughed at that."

"Why?" Abby asks.

"They didn't remodel a thing. It was all new. The Hemlock's place was leveled and up went the big house that is there today. Nice place. But it was not a remodel."

"Did you go inside?" Jack pries.

"Oh, no. Not allowed. I went in the barn. We weren't

the only ones. Half the barn was a love shack. Only a few animals. I could hear others going at it. Kind of turned me on, so we went another round and then I left and went home. But the rumors after. Oh, my."

"Such as?" Abby takes her turn to push for more.

"People disappear sometimes. Teens mostly. I think they're run away. But people around here are suspicious. They think that cult up there has something to do with it."

"And you?" Jack asks.

"Me? No, I think they're kids that don't like the small town life and hitch it to New York or Boston or some other big city. But I'm not the norm, in more ways than one." He says the last with a wink at Jack. "But they are strange. Keep to themselves. Farm their own food and raise cattle. Sometimes they bring in the extra to the food bank. Good stuff. So no, the town and the cult keep their distance. I'm sorry, I'm rambling and your dinner is probably ready and getting cold. I should go check. I really didn't think anyone was coming in tonight and I had a couple drinks. Please don't say anything. I'm afraid the boss would, well…"

"Fire you?" Jack says sternly.

"Yes."

"You're secret is safe with us." Abby says with a fake smile that is convincing enough for the waiter.

"I'll check on your dinner and be right back with fresh drinks, on me. Thank you. Really, thank you for being so understanding." The boy rushes off into the back as the hunters look at one another.

"Is that normal?" Abby asks, not sure how to take what just happened.

"No. No, it is not. That, I would have to say, is a first. But it was useful. And I think we should keep the conversation to lighter subjects until we get back to the room. That boy has the step of a ghost. I didn't hear him, and that's not normal either."

✳ ✳ ✳

Jack's eyes take in the brilliant orange of the sun dipping behind the trees that line the back of the hotel.

Like home. The beach. Only its oaks instead of palms that silhouette the sky. I miss it. Never thought I would, but I do. The surfers. The smell of the ocean. Cool nights almost year around.

"It's gorgeous." Abby's voice pulls him from the live painting.

"Yes." The corners of his mouth move up as the girl drops into the chair opposite him. Black and white lines layout the complex that hides Marie. Jack's hand smoothes the drawings out, ends dripping off the table. A finger points to a section of forest to the south of the farmhouse.

"Here. This is where we get in. Twenty yards at the most to the kitchen window. Then into the house." The finger draws a line from the woods to the back of the house. "From there we move through the kitchen into the hall."

"You're sure this is where the vampire is at?"

"Vampires, if that waiter was right."

"Yes. Vampires."

"Look here. This an old stair well down to a basement on the east side of the house. Over here's a root cellar."

"Yes."

"And this void. It has the feel of being something. The

structure, here." Sheets flip as Jack points at the structural drawings under the plans. "These beams run long. They don't stop. There is a void there. A concrete bunker. A tomb." His eyes move to Abby's. Her eyebrow cocks.

"Like the one that young vampire was determined to stay away from."

"Right. And here. Look at the electrical." Papers turn to a diagram of the houses wiring. "There's a wire leading to this spot, but no switch or receptacle. Just ends. I'd bet that's a key pad to get into that little bunker Marie had built. Remember what the waiter said."

"Out of state contractor and work force."

"Right. So no one local knows about this little hide away. And the Halloween party. It was like a big hello to the community, then nothing."

"He called it a cult."

"So did the gal in the recorder's office."

"True. So this is it?"

"Has to be. The other places, the ones that fit the description the fledge gave us, where pretty much farm houses. Nothing special. Not this one though. And the farmers at the other homes have been there for generations. Our waiter went to school with some of them. I know, I asked him when you went to the rest room."

"Now what?"

"We get some sleep. Need to get up early. I checked with the clerk about hiking and there is a trail that will get us about a quarter mile from the tree line we need to be at. National Forest. We park at the trail head. Hike in. Break off from the trail and get into that house."

"That easy?"

"No, but that's the plan. I'm sure there'll be guards. Maybe dogs. But we don't have time to sit around and wait."

"And the keypad?"

"I have something for that too. All the stuff we need to kill her is in the trunk. Had Sal slip it in before we left."

"Good."

"I'll take the floor and you can have the bed." Jack rolls the plans up and places a rubber band around them. He tosses them into a corner as Abby watches.

"If you're willing to wear shorts, we can share the bed. We'll both need to sleep well."

"Are you sure?" The surprise that washes over Jack's face brings a laugh out of the girl.

"I trust that you will keep to your side of the bed. It is quite large." Her hand floats over the king size mattress as Jack shakes his head, the grin on his lips matching the laughter in his eyes.

"I'll do my best to control myself." The laughter comes out. Abby smiles as she pulls shorts and a tee out of her suitcase and walks to the bathroom.

"Let me know when you've changed." She continues to smile as she disappears into the bathroom.

"What an odd girl." Jack's head shakes as he pulls a pair of work out shorts from his own suit case and begins to change.

Chapter 15
Anna

JACK'S EYES OPEN ONTO THE FAINT DAWN FILTERING through the curtains. The soft snore beside him. His eyes widen. He moves, gently, slowly. The snore turns to a snort then to soft breathing. His legs slip from the sheet, touching the thin carpet. Rhythmic breathing, steady, soft continues as he rises from the soft mattress. He looks back. Short hair fanned out across the pillow that is peaking out behind the soft locks. The girl balled, sheet locked in a grip that a medieval knight would envy. He slips sneakers on, grabs the key card and moves for the door. He looks down to see gentle movement of the sheet, where the girl's chest should be. Eyes closed. Breathing calm. The door handle turns, silence as the door moves into the room. Hall light blocked by the bathroom wall. He moves into the hall.

The door pulls shut with a slight click. He turns to see an empty corridor. The morning silence. Calming. Comforting. He looks at the door.

She's in for a tough day. The thought brings a scowl to his lips. *Taking a girl to kill an ancient. One with guards. With other vampires sleeping beside it. This could turn ugly.*

Jack walks into the little breakfast room. His eyes look over the short, plump woman setting out the muffins and fruit on a little counter. A couple couches and a news channel on the TV is all there is in the lounge. A youthful woman yawns behind the check in desk. She waves, the smile friendly, the eyes tired. Then those tired eyes return to something behind the counter.

"Good morning." The plump woman's tobacco weathered voice says in a friendly tone, the smile looking up at Jack matching the words. Jack smiles. "Coffees in the pot, ready to go if that's what you're looking for. Have some fruit and doughnuts and muffins if you want. We get them from the baker down the way."

"Thank you. I think coffee will be fine for now."

"Waiting for the misses?"

"Yeah."

"My hubby told me about you two. Get away from the kids, eh? Good for you. Wish we would have more often." She moves close as the black liquid creeps up the disposable cup.

"First time we've had one." His smile is kind, his tone has an edge.

"Well, I hope you plan on doing something other than staying in the room."

"What makes you think that that was our plan?" His eye cocked. The woman blushes. It's comical on the old woman's face.

"Away from the kids and all." The red cheeks wink at the man as he sits on the couch. He chuckles.

"Oh, I see. No, there's only so much of that. I think we'll be doing some other exercising today."

"Not much to do here in town." The flush disappears and a helpfulness comes over the woman. She slips onto the couch opposite Jack with a grace he wouldn't have expected.

"No. The forest. Some trails we'd like to try. One off the highway just north of here looks good." He watches as her blood drains from her face. "Are you ok?"

"Don't get caught out there after dark." The stammer. Fear.

"I don't understand?"

"Strange things happen in those woods. Well, that's what I hear anyway. People go missing. Don't come back."

"That section of forest isn't that big."

"That's what makes it so...strange. Rumor is it's that cult up there off the highway. Them folks are different. Bad if you ask me." Jack watches the woman's eyes. The fear, mingled with a thrill of having someone listen to her.

"What's so odd about them?" Jack leans forward, playing up the intrigue. Pushing the woman to keep talking.

"Nothing solid you see. Had a big welcome party a few years back. Couple girls went missing. Sheriff went out there, but nothing. Then the out of towner's doing all that work. We have plenty of people that can build houses in the area. But that woman brought in these guys and after a month or so they packed up and left. Some of them stayed here. Strange folk. Didn't say much. Kept to themselves. And the hair. My God. It was thick as a dog's."

Werewolves. Marie brought in werewolves. Jack tells himself.

"Anything else? Other than the hairy guys and the missing girls?" The woman looks him in the eye. Judging him. Eyeing. Searching for the mockery she is expecting. Finds none, grins as her eyes flicker around the room.

"Yeah. They weren't the only ones. And not just girls. Boys too. Men. Women. Animals, too. And the woman that runs the place. Shit she looks more like a little girl, then a woman. Well, she's never out in the daylight. At least not that anyone I know has seen. Not that anyone gets a chance to see anything out there. No, them folk keep to themselves. Like they're hiding something."

"Hiding what?"

"You want to know what I think?" Her voice drops to a whisper. Eyes searching for unwanted ears dropping in.

"Yeah?"

"Satan worshipers. Praying to the devil. That's what I think. They make spirits and beer up there. How they make their money. Grow their own food. Don't buy much in town. And when they do come, it's always in a group. Four at least. Anyway. They talk about odd things too."

"Such as?"

"Vampires. Werewolves."

"Are you serious?" He leans in. Seriousness on his face. The seed of doubt crushed as he waits for her answer.

"Yeah. Most people in town have heard it. The monster talk as some call it. But I do know one thing.

People that go out that way and end up out after dark. Well, they are less likely to come back."

"Well, I'll make sure we get back well before dark." Jack leans back, sips his coffee, watches the woman as she eyes him.

"You don't believe a thing I told you, do you?"

"You would be surprised what I believe. And what I have done. Do you want to know something?" His eyes bore into the woman. She moves forward. Curious.

"Yes."

"I believe you. That they are an odd bunch. That there might be something going on out there. That they may be responsible for people disappearing. That's why I think me and the misses will get out of town after our little hike." The woman's jaw sags. She stammers.

"I didn't mean that you needed to get out of town."

"No, I think that would be best. Anyway. The misses is missing the kids and is not in the mood for anymore adventures. We may even skip the hike. But I thank you for the story. And believe me. I don't think you are as crazy as you think I do." His smile is gentle, kind. It softens the scowl that is forming on the woman's face. Turning it to a gentle grin.

"You're messing with me."

"Kind of. But we are leaving tonight. The misses is wanting to get back. And work is getting backed up for me. I think we'll call it a short vacation this time." His chuckle pulls a full belly laugh out of the old woman. She winks and moves to the coffee pot, pouring a cup for herself then moving into the back room. Jack's smile drops as the woman disappears behind the curtain.

So, even the towns folk think something is up. Satanists. Makes sense. Easier to believe than vampires and werewolves or whatever other monsters might be roaming into that little compound. We need to be extra cautious. Don't know what exactly we are getting ourselves into.

Jack stands. Walks to the counter. Fills his cup. Fills one with water, adds a tea bag and walks back to the room.

Need to get Abby up and going. This might be a bad one.

Chapter 16
Abby

JACK'S ELBOW CRADLES HIS COFFEE AS THE PLASTIC CARD slips into the slot on the door. A click. The handle pulls down. A heavy push. The light of the sun illuminates the room, bringing a golden hue to everything in it. The bathroom door is closed. Light sneaking out from the space between the carpet and the door. Shuffling of clothes. Quiet. A bare foot stepping closer to the door. Quiet.

"It's me." Jack calls to the unseen Abby. "I got you a cup of tea and there's muffins and such down the hall."

"Thank you. I should only be a few more minutes in here."

"Sure. We should get going soon. Get there early. Get on the road while we still have a good amount of daylight."

Jack sets the drinks on the table beside the rolled up plans. He unrolls them. Looks them over. Looks up at the click of the bathroom door. Abby walks toward him. Shorts that land just above mid thigh, a tank top. The pink sports bra peaking out from under the equally pink top.

"I'm ready. Are you going like that?" She slips the tea, looks down at the plans.

"No. Need to get dressed."

"I'll wait in here."

"Sure." Jack pulls his things out of his bag, moves to the bathroom.

He slips out of the workout shorts and into a pair of cargo shorts. Changes the tee and puts on tennis shoes. He can hear the girl. The one that he is to teach how to kill vampires. The sound of her fingers moving through the plans.

Studying. Good. A slight smile creeps across his face. *She is learning.* The clothes are gathered from the floor and he tosses them in his bag.

"Bring the suitcases and let's get out of here."

"We're not coming back?" Questioning on her face. She looks at him.

"No. No need. We should be done in the morning. Then get on the road. Put distance between us and the lair. What'll soon be a crime scene. We'll have to burn it down. Destroy the lair completely. It'll be on the news if we do this right and I'd rather not be around for police questions."

"I understand."

"Good."

"And the hotel?"

"I told them you miss the kids." Jack chuckles.

"Yes, that would be appropriate." Abby's head nods slightly. A sadness there that Jack hasn't seen.

"What is it?"

"I can't have children."

"I'm sorry."

"It was something that happened long ago. It doesn't bother me." He watches her turn, the blank expression disappearing in a blur of hair.

She's lying.

"Oh." His voice trails off as Abby opens the door, turning, eyes taking in the uncertainty in his face.

"We should get moving." A slight nod to the hall. A squint of unknowing. Then she moves from view, hidden by the wall that separates them.

Jack jogs to catch up. Watches as she places the bag in the trunk. Turns to him. Waits, impatience in the twitch of her lip. He tosses in his suitcase. Walks to the door, slips behind the wheel. Silence. He looks at her. Eyes forward. The engine rumbles. The click of the shifter as it slips into gear. The crunch of gravel and then onto the road leading them through the little town, north. To the vampire's lair.

"How?" The softness of his voice pulls her eyes to him, questioningly. A wonder in them.

"How what?" The cocked head of curiosity beside him as his eyes remain on the road speeding past them.

"How did you lose the ability to have children?"

"I was in an accident." Her voice flattens as she looks forward, avoiding him.

"Where you young?"

"Fourteen. It was a horse that kicked me. Hard. It

damaged my pelvis and when the doctors did surgery they found that my uterus was ruptured."

"They couldn't fix it?"

"No. It was bad. The bone had ripped through me. I was in bed for a year. I studied. A lot."

"And?"

"And I learned to live with the loss of having children. Of being infertile. It was a shock to my Aunt. Me being the only living relative left in the family. I was not concerned."

"Oh."

"You seem disappointed." Her eyes take in the blank expression on his face. The hiding of his feelings. A talent he has honed over the years.

"No, just surprised. Most women I know think that children are part of their future."

"I never wanted children. Never. Even as a girl. I wanted knowledge. To learn."

"And now?"

"I'm sorry?"

"You are becoming a hunter."

"Ah, yes. It is still learning. And I plan to continue my research even as we hunt the vampires."

"Alright."

"I think the turn is here." Abby's finger points at the trailhead off the side of the road. The empty dirt lot is shaded from the morning sun by the oaks that enclose the trail.

"Yep." Jack nods, grateful to move away from the conversation. To have something physical to occupy his mind.

The car stops at the edge of the trees. He steps out as Abby shuts her door. The trunk pops open with a pull of fingers on the lever. Jack looks up to see Abby pulling out the packs. He takes his, locks the car and they move under the trees.

"How long until we get to the farm?" Her voice is quiet, secretive.

"Half hour or so. We go off the trail at that bend."

Silence covers them as the faint crunch of leaves and branches muffles in the trees. They move quietly and quickly. Letting the sounds of the forest mask their footfalls. Birds sing. A wood pecker hammers far in the distance. Squirrels scamper through the branches. The smell of a light rain from the night before drifts up from the moist ground. The damp providing more cover for their sneakers. Jack stops. Looks. The trees thin ahead. He moves, crouched, silent.

An opening shows the farmhouse. White. Two stories. Picturesque. Binoculars come out of his pack. He scans. Focuses on the guard moving slowly across the grounds. Passing the kitchen window, the one they need to use to gain entry to the house. The guard stops. Pulls a cigarette from his shirt pocket. Lights it. Scans the tree line. Takes a deep pull, causing the cherry to blaze, even in the bright of day. Then he moves toward the barn. A young woman walks toward him. A wink. A nod to the barn. He grins. They slip into the shadows. A ten foot door swings closed. Jack looks at Abby. Her own spy glasses fixed on the barn. He scans again. Nothing. His glasses slip back into his pack.

"What now?" Abby's whisper is barely heard above the rustle of leaves.

"We wait." The words are slow, determined.

Eyes look at magnified windows and doors. The sound of a dog in the distant. The movement of another guard, leaning against the house, a trail of smoke from the cigarette dangling off the edge of slightly chapped lips. His glass eyes show the youthful face, smooth where stubble will one day be. Another, gruff and older marches close, anger in the almost black eyes that are surrounded by dark skin.

Jack lets the words move over his eyes, the lips of the men telling him all he needs to know. A slacker and his boss, or so that is what the older man would have the younger believe. The youth shrugs, the indifference only building the older mans anger.

There is hate in those eyes. Murder even. Jack looks at the girl beside him.

"They're going to be our distraction. It's easy sometimes." Jack leans back against a tree, lets the trunk take his weight as he watches, without the aid of the binoculars, as the grumbles turns to anger that is beyond the older man's control.

"What do you mean easy?" The sound of her voice, soft in the tree line. The shade giving a pleasant feel to the horrid things that are to come. Jack smiles. Not a friendly smile, it is tight, hard.

"Vampires tend to hire on those that put themselves first. Have little regard for others. Let's just say they tend to be full of their own worth. Those types don't work well together. Soon, those two men over there are going to come to blows. Possibly more, if that kid really pisses off that guy."

"How can you tell? It just looks like an argument. Won't one of them just walk away?" Abby's eyes follow the men. The older moving closer to the youth, still leaning on the building, smoke drifting from the dwindling cigarette.

"No, they'll fight. I've seen it before. Most times it's just a fist fight. But that guy, there is more to it. The kid screwed his girl. The kid insulted him. There is a promise of the kid becoming a vampire. Hell, could be that one of the vampires gave the kid more attention and the old guy feels slighted. But what I can see is a very pissed off dude that is about to take on a kid half his age."

"And then what?"

"We use it. We take the fight and the aftermath. A brawl brings out a crowd and focuses their attention on the fighters. We use it and we get in that little window we saw on the plans. The kitchen is beyond. We sneak in. Get to that little panel, the door beside the stairs, and get into that basement. The one that isn't on the plans. Get down there and do what we came here for. Until then we wait."

"Ok." Abby's voice is soft. Almost hurt. Ignored is what Jack would guess.

"Do you want to talk?" His low voice just louder than the yells from across the field. Out of the corner of his eye he can see others moving toward the argument. The barn couple move out, clothes being buttoned up as the crowd around the two men grows.

"Yes? Why do you hate vampires so much? I despise them, but you know my reasons. Why do you?" The words are gentle, caring, but firm. He studies her face. Emotionless. But the eyes. There is wonder there. The first time he has really noticed it. She wants to know.

"I have my reasons. The one I hunt..."

"Tristen?"

"Yes, Tristen. That one took from me something that can never be replaced. Something so dear to me that I feel the pain of its loss everyday."

"What was it?"

"Something dear. Maybe one day I'll tell you. Let you know the reason. But not today. What I will tell you is that these creatures are a danger to all mankind. They are hunters that seek out human life and then snuff it out like a cheap candle. That is another reason I do this. So that there is one less person, one less family, that has to feel the pain that I have felt. Sadly, most people never know that it was a vampire that killed their loved one."

"Yes, they do cover their tracks well." She whispers louder as the sound of a crack jolts the hunters out of their conversation.

"You son of a bitch!" The growl of the older man is clear as he rushes the youth, eyes wide as he realizes that he has made the wrong move.

"Told you they'd fight." Jack's dry voice has none of the loftily arrogance in it, just a fact acknowledged.

The men are at each other. Guards, sitting in the house move out to the porch. Jack raises the binoculars, peers into the house. Let's them move over the interior, shades open but windows closed.

"There's no movement in the house now. They're all outside watching those idiots pummel each other."

"What now?" Abby asks, a little to innocently.

"We get in that house."

"How?"

"Sprint to the window. You go in first. Then me."

"And if some one is in there?"

"We check first. But those assholes are going to be at it for a bit and that crowd isn't going anywhere."

Her nod is barely seen as Jack's legs send him across the twenty yards that separate the forest from the kitchen. He chances a look behind. Abby's small frame keeps pace. He slides. Leans against the wall below the window. Steadies his breath. Moves up, looks in, slips back down.

"Well?"

"Nothing. It's empty. They're all outside like I thought." He stands. Pushes the window up. The space is just enough for his larger build, Abby slips in easily. He follows.

Chapter 17
Marie

"THE HALL IS THIS WAY." JACK'S VOICE IS SUBDUED. "Remember that they're right outside so keep it down." A slight tapping of the tennis shoes on the tile floor is barely heard over the shouts of the fight and of those that watch. Moving around the kitchen island, the stovetop centered across from the sink the pair climbed over. He stops. Hand motions for silence. The squeak of wood stressing metal. A bare foot appears between the step and the wall. A woman. Workout shorts. Cropped tee. Anger on her pretty face.

"What the fuck is going on out there? Can't anyone let a girl sleep?" The words have a mix of sleep and anger in them.

She moves toward the door, trying to get a look at the ruckus that has awoken her. She yawns as bare feet move slowly, bringing her closer to the closed door. It's wide wood shape blocking the brawl outside. The sound of fist to flesh coming through the wall. A mingle of cheers mix the the fighting sounds. Curses, the spitting of a tooth to the ground. Angry words draw the women closer.

Jack creeps across the hall. His body pushes against the stair, slips behind the sleepy woman. His hand moves fast. The palm covers the woman's mouth. Her elbow flashes back into the hunter's stomach. A grunt from Jack and his fingers dig into the woman's cheeks. His other arm moving fast, wraps around her waist and pulls her against him. She kicks at him, twisting to try to get out of the vice like grip he has on her.

His hand shifts slightly on the woman's mouth. He jerks, fast and hard. A slight snap pops out of the neck as the woman's body stiffens then her full weight is taken by the arm holding her waist. Jack moves the limp body to the kitchen. Sits it behind the wall. Let's it sink into to marble tile. He turns, moves to the girl he is training and looks at her wide eyed stare.

"Won't they find her? Sound the alarm?" He can hear the panic in her voice. He looks at her firmly, a reassurance in his eyes.

"We should be done by then, this part goes fast. There's only four of them and they are asleep in that tomb of theirs. If not, then we're going to have worse problems than a few pissed off human guards.

"Ok, sorry." The remorse in her voice. The sound of her feeling failure.

"Don't worry. But we need to get this done before those two tire themselves out or one of them lands a lucky punch. Let's go." The sound of Jack's voice barely audible in Abby's ears.

He moves at a crouch, slips around the corner. His head bobs past the railing. He turns to look at her.

"It's quiet up there." Jack whispers.

The bark of a dog brings their heads around to the front of the house. The sound of cheers and the fight come through the closed door. Jack's hand glides across the white wood panel below the stair. It stops. Pushes. A slight click. A panel, small, pops open. A button stares back at him. His eyes move across the room. They focus on Abby, her attention on the opening to the little nook beside the stairs.

If they get us here, we're trapped.

A finger depresses the button. Another click, louder, though not by much. A panel swings slightly into the room. Quietly. The smell of cool air slips through the hidden door. The panel joint masking the jamb.

"You ready?" His eyes focused out the girl as he pulls a flashlight from his pack, a short silver sword in the other hand.

"Yes." Her voice is stronger than he would have excepted. The grip on her flashlight and dagger showing white at the knuckles betraying the sound that passes from her lips.

"Quiet. We go in. Heads only, then burn it down. I'll take two and you take two."

Jack's hand moves the door open. Concrete stairs greet them. And darkness. The smell of earth. A wave of cool hits the hunters as they step into the inky black, flashlights scanning the open wood framing. Wiring, gas and water lines. All weave around the light frame. The smell of earth grows. Jack's boot touch the soft ground.

He moves in. Can hear the dirt shuffle under his feet. His light moves slowly, taking in the unfinished basement. Stops. Set on the row of concrete slabs. Four pale white forms stretched out in the sleep of the undead. He moves closer. The creatures lay in night clothes. All female. All in white gowns that come to their knees. All have the look of youth.

The towns folk were wrong about the males. Jack realizes.

Jack's eyes move over them. All the colors of the hair there. Blonde, brown, black and red. Which one is the leader, he can't tell. He moves in, motioning to Abby to take the opposite side. He looks at her. The light shining from the position of her mouth, teeth hold the metal flashlight in place. A nod from the man and the swords come down in a swish of air. The ring of metal on stone as the heads roll off the slabs and thud into the dirt. Swords raise again, drop, and the second pair of heads roll onto the dirt. Jack pulls his flashlight out of his mouth. Scans the little room. There is nothing here but the decapitated vampires. The dirt floor. The unfinished walls. Vampiric blood soaking concrete and earth. No secrets. No other vampires. Nothing. He pulls cooking jelly from his bag, slips on rubber gloves and pops the lid to the jelly. He smears it on the exposed wood. On the metal pipes feeding the gas to the floors above. He looks over to see that Abby is doing the same. A grim smile touches his lips, then it disappears as he finishes with the last can.

"We need to get out of here. Get to the woods. Get up there and see if it is still clear. I hope those two are still at it." The soft whisper brings her into action.

Silent steps up the concrete stairs in the dark. Jack pulls the candle lighter out of his bag. Tosses the bag over one of the vampire's bodiless heads and waits.

"All clear." The sound of Abby's voice just heard.

The lighter ignites the jelly. It spreads. Fast. Jack is at the steps as he looks behind. The light framing is engulfed in blue red flame. The metal that controls the flammable gas within the pipes begins to buckle slightly from the heat. Two at a time he takes the stairs. Stops at the top. Abby looks at him, he nods toward the kitchen. Bravado curses from the tired combatants on the other side of the front door meet his ears. The hunters rush out as the smoke begins to bellow out of the vampire's lair. They stop at the window. The sound of movement. Soft mumbles. The fight is over and they need to get out of the house.

"Fire!" A woman's voice from the opposite side of the house.

The sound of yells. Commands, maybe. Jack can't make it out. He peeks into the expanse between him and woods. Nothing. No-one. He slips out of the window, drops to the grass below. Scans. The sounds of turmoil louder. Someone is trying to take charge. Abby drops down beside him. No sign of the guards. They sprint. Jack looking back to see if any of the guards have spotted them. He sees the focus is on the smoke bellowing out of the house. The kitchen window now has smoke coming out of it. A pair of women stumble out of the front door. Coughing. Others help. Screams from the upper floors. The humans that live there begin to feel the flames.

"Wait." Jack pulls Abby beside him. The forest shields them from the eyes of the compound members.

"Why?"

"We need to make sure." He watches. Garden hoses pour water in a hopeless attempt. The screams die out. The explosion, as gas lines brake, throws the water bearers to the ground. The house sags. Taking an unnatural shape. Then it collapses. Fire consuming it. The few people watching are in tears. Some are angry, most are in shock.

Jack pulls at the girl. Nods for them to go. They move low in the forest undergrowth. Raising up as the sounds of fear and anger can no longer be heard. They walk in silence to the trail. Stop. Look for fellow hikers. None. Move out onto the trail and head back to the car.

"What now?" Abby asks as she slips into the passenger seat.

"We go back to your Aunt and I find out where Tristen is." Jack growls as he pulls the car onto the road.

Chapter 18
Carol

JACK STRETCHES OUT ON HIS SINGLE BED. THE BLANKET wrinkled beneath his clothed body. Cool air blowing in from the vent above him, helping with the wet summer air. The walls of his room are bare of any adornment. The off-white paint reflecting the sunlight that glows from the single window of the small chamber that is all his. A sense of ease sinks into his very being.

Vampires don't walk around in the daylight. The smile on his lips curls the edges of his mouth as the thought embeds itself in his mind. Closing his eyes, he lets the past few days sink in. Carlos, Ingrid, the hotel, Abby, Carol, and all the rest. The smile disappears as past days continue to flash in his mind.

It's been a whirlwind. He thinks as he takes a deep breath, letting it out slowly, the tension melting.

How did I end up here. A group of scholars. Researchers. None of them knows the reality of the things they study. The girl, Abby. She's smart. Strong in her own way. But her experience,

| 163 |

it's all books. Not knowing about stakes. Simple stuff, falling through the cracks of academia. And this Aunt. She's dangerous. More so than any of these people know. I've seen the type. Regal. Self important. Acting though they are not. No, this one needs to be watched. But the girl. Not wanting the role of hunter. Needing her books. The tomb of knowledge below us. She'll do well, that's for sure, but there's no passion. Passion, funny. Killing shouldn't be passionate, even if you are killing monsters that prey on the foolish and weak. No, that's not it. It's not passion. Not for me. It's revenge. Seeking to destroy the things that nearly destroyed me. That's the truth. Something I've always know. But something I rarely face.

Jack's eyes move to the sound of air forced through the vent above the window. The hum is comforting. His eyes grow heavy as the cool air pushes past the exposed skin, bringing up goose bumps. The corners of his mouth turn up ever so slightly.

This is nice. Nicer than anything I've felt in a long time. Quiet. A comfortable bed. Little concern of some unnatural thing breaking in and trying to rip my heart out. No. This is nice. Surrounded by others that know what is out there. That are watching for the odd thing that might creep in through the black of night. Nice. Nice to be in a place that is filled with a protection that I've not felt since she died.

The smile disappears as painful thoughts push the pleasant ones aside. His eyes open. Head turns to the door as the knuckles softly contact the heavy oak. He lays still, waiting for the sound to disappear. For the intruder of his solitude to be ignored away. The rap is louder. His sigh is all but silent. Socked feet touch the floor. Find his boots. Slip inside the leather. Another rap, louder still.

"Mr. Simpson?" The sound of a young man's nervous voice breaks the well-deserved silence.

"Come in." Jack ties the work boots laces as the other foot falls to the floor, its laces in place.

"Sir, Miss Vinson would like to see you." The flush of the boys face brings questions to Jack's mind.

"Abby?"

"No, sir. It is the mistress that wishes to see you. She has asked that I escort you to her chambers. She has had the chef prepare lunch." There is fear in the boys voice. His eyes darting everywhere.

"What is it?" The calm of Jack's voice only heightens the boys nerves.

"Sir?" A squeak.

"You're nervous. What is it?"

"You. You're a hunter?"

"Yes."

"You've killed?" The break in the boys voice reminds Jack of how young he must be.

"How old are you?"

"Sixteen, sir."

"Sixteen. And what are you doing here?"

"I help with chores, sir."

"No. What are you doing here. You're sixteen. You should be in high school. Chasing girls. Getting good or bad grades. So why are you here?"

"I'm an orphan, sir. My parents." The words trail off uncomfortably.

"Yes?"

"They were hunters, sir." The clinch of the boys voice

affects the words, tightens the speech. The eyes turn away. Jack can see the discomfort.

"And they died." The statement brings the boys eyes back to face the man standing beside him. Looking him in the eye. Their heights so much the same.

"Yes."

"How?"

"Sir?"

"How did they die? What killed them?" Jack's hand sits on the boys shoulder, comforting him, allowing him to face the question.

"A vampire, sir."

"I see. And now you seek to learn about them. To do what? Destroy them?"

"No. I just want others to be safe from their acts of destruction. To stop the murders."

"And that, young man, is a better reason than the one that I have chosen. But, I think that I should keep my demons to myself."

"Yes, sir."

"Lead the way to the, what did you call her, oh yeah, the mistress of the house." Jack's sliver of a smile returns. The boy, seeing the upturned lips giggles with the nervousness of a teenager that is not sure how to act around his crazy uncle.

"Yes, sir." The lighter tone, the ease, Jack can hear in the boys words.

"And another thing. Don't call me sir. Call me Jack. Everyone else does."

"Yes…uh…Jack." The boy stutters with a smile of getting away with a small crime.

Jack's laughter, only felt on the inside, brings a happiness to him that erases the pain that had been forming in his room. The boy leads him through the corridors to a pair of heavy oak doors. He knocks and is summoned. Inside, Carol sits at a small table. Set as if for a five star restaurant. The boy closes the door behind him and Jack looks at the ancient looking woman, her smile brings out the wrinkles that etch her skin.

"Have a seat Mr. Simpson, we have much to discuss." The slow movement ends with her liver spot speckled hand pointing at the seat opposite herself.

Jack nods and moves to the plump chocolate colored chair. He sinks slightly into the comfortable seat and looks across at the woman as she sips ice tea, the cubes shifting as the glass moves up and the liquid touches her lips.

"I've completed your little task." The words are harsh, gruff.

He sees the table laid out before him. Two places. Plates, a full water glass, flatware that appears to be silver. The white table cloth contrasting with the dark hues of the chairs and the navy blue suit his summoner wears. The white pearls around her neck match the table covering and the plates. A pale blue blouse completes the outfit. His eyes take all this in. Her smile, possibly forced, looks back at him.

"Yes. You have completed the task that I have set out for you. You have taught my niece much in the ways of hunting of vampires." The smile remains. Her movements are slow, calculated as the glass of tea sets on the table.

"And now I would like to know where Tristen is." His hands set on the table, he leans forward. The malice on his face removes the smile from the woman's face. A slight sigh escapes her lips, a sigh of frustration.

"Yes. Tristen. As per our agreement. I will provide you with the details of his location. As much as we have. But first I would offer a proposal."

"And what might that be?" Jack moves back as a young woman, fourteen at the most, brings in Caesar salads.

Carol smiles at the girl as she places them on the plates, turns and walks away without a word. Jack follows her with his eyes. Then turns to Carol as the door closes, leaving them in solitude.

"My niece. She still has much to learn. Much that needs to be experienced." Her fork stabs through a crouton and leaf of lettuce. She moves the morsel to her mouth.

"You want me to train her. That's not the deal. Deal was to kill that vampire up north and then I go my own way." Jack's salad remains untouched, his eyes bore into Carol as she chews.

"You are correct. I was hoping that we could come to another arrangement. One that would benefit us both. One that would help my niece improve her skills."

"Why?"

"Oh, my dear Mr. Simpson, isn't it clear that the girl needs training." The smirk annoys Jack as she pats the corners of her lips with the white napkin, staining it with dressing.

"Not the training. Why are you having her do this? She doesn't want it. Books are her thing. She'd be happier down in that tomb of yours. So why are you pushing her into the field? Why are you making her a hunter when she has no passion for it?"

"You care for her. I did not see that as a possibility."

"You thought I had no heart. That I was so cold that I would not be able to feel for another human being?"

"No, of course not. It is my niece. She tends to be off putting. Her personality is, well, let's say odd."

"Yes. But she's smart. Very smart. And a quick study."

"Yes. That is one of her strengths. And that is why she must train to be a hunter."

"I still don't understand."

"To run a house, as I do, you must have field experience. Hunting is the best type, though other investigative types will do."

"You want to turn this over to her."

"Yes. She is the natural choice."

"There isn't someone else?"

"No, she has been groomed for this. It was decided long ago by members of the board. You didn't think that this was something I would want for her. Oh no, Mr. Simpson. I would have rather she went to a boarding school in the city. That she would move on to university and study whatever subject that she had a passion for. I assure you. This was not my choice."

"I see. And this board? Why did they choose her?"

"She has a way of seeing things. Has had this unique perspective since she was a child. It is something that the board feels will help us in our future endeavors."

"But first she must be trained."

"Yes."

"And if I am not interested?"

"Then I will be forced to find a less suitable replacement."

"So it's happening regardless."

"Yes."

"Does she know?"

"No. And it must not be revealed until the proper time."

"Ok, I can do that."

"You are willing to continue to train her?"

"Yes. At least until I kill Tristen."

"And then?"

"I don't know. But for now Tristen is my focus."

"I believe I can assist you with that. He is in Miami. He has a compound. We do not have the exact location. You will still need to do some detective work. I will provide the financial needs, as you will still be considered under our protection. Abby will arrange transportation, lodging and weapons. She will be your assistant. You will be in charge."

"When can we leave?"

"Your flight leaves this afternoon. You will be in Miami by five."

"You expected me to agree to this."

"Yes. It was a risk worth taking, Mr. Simpson. Your exploits are well known. Having you as an ally in this fight, and it is becoming a fight, Mr. Simpson, gives us an advantage. I wish you good hunting."

Jack bites into his salad. Savoring the flavor and remembering how hungry he is. The pair remain silent as they finish their meal. Eyes remaining fixed on the plates in front of them. The silence is relaxing. The tension melting away like the butter on the warm bread the youthful girl has brought for them. Jack looks up to see the smile has returned to the old woman's face. It has a warmth that wasn't there before. He pats his mouth clean with the napkin, watching her.

"What is it?" His words warm, caring.

"You remind me of someone I cared deeply for when I was younger. I think that may be why it has been difficult to deal with you on such a professional level. But that being said, I must return to my duties. It is not all luncheons and coffees. I have a branch to run. I do wish you success with the elimination of Tristen. He is a vampire that we have watched for years. He is also one that tends to disappear and then reappear."

Carol stands slowly. Age showing in the movements. The smile becomes strained with whatever pain jolts her body. She straightens, smiles at him, and walks to the door opposite him. She turns as the door opens. Another hall leading to more rooms.

"Please look after Abby. She can be naive."

"Yes, that is something I have noticed."

Carol disappears behind the closed door and Jack finishes his warm bread. The tinge of sourdough pleasant on his tongue.

Chapter 19

Abby

"Jack." Abby's voice floats through the dim hall.

He turns to see the girl almost jogging to reach him. A seriousness to her face, that is all but common to him now. This time there's something different, something intense about the girl's look. The wrinkled brow and the slight huff of breath. He waits as she closes the distance between them. Her features growing clearer. The sundress, hitting mid thigh, ending its running dance.

"What is it?" The concern in his voice brings her to a stop.

"I wanted to meet with you before we have to leave, before we go to the airport." Her tone steadies.

She looks up at him, then behind her. The movement is suspense in action. He watches, one eyebrow raised.

"What are you up too?" The words come out slow and deliberate.

"We need to go to the archive. I need to show you what I have found. It's about Tristen, the vampire you want to kill. He's, well, much older than you thought." The anxiety, something he's not seen in her, bubbles out in her words. A tinge of fear in the shifting eyes.

"Is this something that is suppose to be a secret. You're not going to get in trouble with your Aunt are you?" The concern is real.

Then it hits him. He hasn't had feelings for another, not since Beth, but that was a long time ago. And she's, well, going to be another problem to deal with sooner than later. And it's not the same kind of feelings that he had. There's not the sexual aspect to it. More of a fatherly thing. He chuckles inside as she explains that it's ok, but time is short. Then she leads him through the halls to a stairway that leads down into the earth covered basement.

"It's down here, the library. Sealed from the rear of the building. Everything is concrete and the humidity is kept low. Some of these books and scrolls are thousands of years old."

"How did you get them?" His hand slides along the cool metal railing taking him down into the library. She moves ahead of him. Feet making no sound.

"We've had them for a long time. Collected when the Society formed. Many of the men that began the order were learned men. Scholars and professors. Men that had such things in their possession. It was when they died that the books became the beginnings of a library. There are many. Some of the books are one of a kind. But all have been entered into the computers. No internet here, you have to link directly into the server to see the files, to read the books. The books themselves are not to be touched, just achieves." The words rush out of her, a glow of happiness beams from her face as she looks back at the hunter behind her. Her slim hand turns the knob of the door and Jack is greeted with a pair of computers facing one another.

"Just the two?"

"Yes. Research is limited. Access is rarely given."

"So how did you get into the system?"

"I'm an archivist. I have unlimited access. That was a condition of accepting your training. I would be allowed to continue my studies here." She slips into the leather desk chair. Lets the screen come to life and taps onto the keyboard. "I'll bring up what I found. It was buried. I doubt anyone has seen it since it was entered into the system."

"And you only have the one server? What if something did happen?" Jack learns over the girl's shoulder watching the files load.

"Back ups are made daily. And we transfer back ups to other houses once a month. The most we would lose is a months worth of work."

"I see."

"Here it is."

"What am I looking at?"

"It's Tristen. An early photo from around eighteen ninety. The description says he is the owner of a small night club. Women had gone missing in the area and he was interviewed by the police, being a business owner." Jack takes in the photo.

The man's dark hair and period dress as he stands outside of a nightclub. The wood sign announcing the beer and whiskey that is offered within. It is dark and the flash of the bulb washes the rest of the surroundings into black.

"Looks like it was taken at night." Jack points to the blackened back ground.

"Yes. There is more. This was just one account of your vampire. There are more. A few news clippings about him" She looks up, sees the pain in his eyes. "What is it?"

"I'll tell you on the plane. Ask me then. Right now I want to know what you've found."

"He's been around for a long time. In the US for at least two hundred years. Before that it seems he lived in England. At least another two hundred years. See this here." A finger points to the list of names that go from one man to the next. At the top of the list is scrawled the word Tristen. Under it, in the same handwriting is:

> *Ancient vampire, list of assumed names listing back to 1678. Names end here. Some evidence shows that the vampire may have come from the middle east, though there is little to support this. I feel this is one of the older vampires still in existence. He may be the key to learning how these creatures came to be. Some lore that only one this old would know. I have searched for him and found nothing. The trail of names goes cold in 1958. Not sure if the creature was killed or just found a better method of hiding his identity. Either way this is the list of names below. Maybe a future researcher will find it useful and continue the search for this ancient.*

Jack scans the names, dating back to the late sixteen hundreds. All English and American locations. He looks at Abby, he eyes on her.

"We need to get to the plane and get down to Miami. This has to end." The gruff in his voice brings her to action. The computer goes dark with a flick of a switch and the pair rush up the stairs.

Chapter 20
Jack

THE RIDE TO THE AIRPORT WAS A QUIET ONE. PAIN BROUGHT up by the photos of Tristen, seeing his vampiric form again. Jack's eyes looked out the tinted window of the limo, trying to let his mind let go of the anger and hate. The images brought to the front of his mind. Seeing trees that line the highway toward the city blurred past letting his mind drift as he sat beside the girl that he agreed to teach the dark art of killing monsters. The trees soon turn to the suburban landscape that all cities seem to have in common. Jack can feel the tug on his body as the limo pulls into one of these suburbs. He looks at his partner. The cocked eye asking for information. A thin smile of uncertainty beams back at him from the young face.

"We are going to a small airport. Private. It is outside of the city. We have a private jet. I have it arranged for us to be in Miami by early evening." The smile disappears as Jack's eyes drift back to the ever changing blurred window scene.

He watches the limo pull into the drop off and moves through the light line of cars. The concourse is small. Lined with windows that provide a view of the aircraft on the tarmac. Small ones, not the large liners that are found at the large airports, the only ones he has ever been too. A perforated metal sunshade juts out over the road and sidewalk, providing some relief from the sun. His thoughts move to the lack of protection from rain and snow as the car stops at the curb with a slight jolt. He looks at the back of the drivers obscured head. The fogged window that separated him from his passengers obscures the man's features. The click of the trunk brings the hunter back to the here and now.

Jack lets himself out of the car, feeling the breeze of Abby's door open. He steps around to the trunk. The youth behind the wheel jogs to the popped hatch and pulls out the three bags of luggage. Jack forces a smile at the youth. The one he spoke to. Jack wonders how many youth the Society has working for it. The free labor. The thought slips away as the youth returns to the drivers seat and pulls the limo away, leaving Jack with Abby standing on the curb, bags in hand.

"The plane is this way." Her voice is matter of fact. The emotion gone. Caution returning. He notes that it's a defensive thing. Something she has trained herself to do over the years. It makes sense to him after seeing the world she was raised in. Stiff, precise, adult.

"No check in?" He rolls his bag and shoulders her lighter one as she rolls her larger bag into the cool air conditioned lobby. The smell of bleach and disinfectant attacks his nostrils. He looks around at the others in the place. Wealth surrounds him. Staff shuffle around those that think they are somehow better due to their money, trying to remain hidden from their gaze. Jack hates this. The wealth privilege. The act of feeling that you deserve something for the size of your bank account. It sickens him and he follows the quick pace that Abby has set through the lobby out onto the tarmac. A woman waves to her. A smile on her face. A friendliness that Jack hasn't encountered since leaving Armand.

"Abby. So good to see you again." The woman is young, though not a teen. Possibly in her twenties, Jack observes as a young man takes the bags from Abby and himself and loads them into the small jet.

"Yes, it has. I see you have been promoted to pilot." Abby's words are soft, tender. In a way that Jack hasn't heard her use them with anyone but himself. A smile sneaks across his face at the thought that the girl does have friends. That her youth was not as lonely as he assumed.

"And this must be Jack the vampire hunter. The one I have heard so much about. Well let's get you two on board and get you to Miami before the sun goes down." The blonde nods toward the plane, as the man remove the blocks from the tires. "It should be a couple hours flight. We have snacks and drinks. Mario will be doing most of the flying, he's in training to become a pilot as well." The smile charms even Jack as the trio move up the steps into the cabin.

Inside is typical of a high-end jet. Cozy chairs. Real tables. Carpeted floors. A bar at the rear of the plane. A young woman in a blue uniform that matches the pilots, waits beside the drink service silently.

Jack follows Abby to a table, sits opposite her as the pilot moves into the cockpit. The co-pilot pulls the door into position, the clunk of the locking mechanism ensures it is closed.

"What is it?" Jack's voice barely heard over the sound of the engines warming for the flight.

"I thought the photos would help." The hurt is there, but it is hard to read.

"They did."

"Then why…" Her words trail with uncertainty.

"Why did I become upset?" His sad smile softens her. "Yes?"

"I looked at the face of the monster that killed my wife. Did your Aunt tell you that. That it was Tristen that did this. That thing made me what I am?" His hand touches hers. The touch is soft, with a kindness that she accepts. Still the eyes remain focus elsewhere.

"No. But I would like to know." The hurt in her eyes turns to compassion as they turn to look at his own. An emotion he assumes is not one she is comfortable with.

"It was a long time ago. I was in San Diego. Working as an architect. Late nights were common back then. It was one of those nights when my wife was killed." Jack pauses, lets the memories wash over him. The pain. The anger. He takes a deep breath, smiles as the stewardess steps up beside them.

"Would you care for anything? We have full bar and a cheese platter if you would like." The words are friendly, but rehearsed. The woman's tone is uncaring.

"Coffee and the cheese platter." Jack's words are softer than his mood. Abby smiles politely and asks for water with the cheese. The stewardess turns as the fasten seat belts sign flashes on.

"She is new." Abby's tone is apologetic.

"That's fine." Jack watches the woman buckle into a seat as the plane moves along the tarmac.

Abby watches him. The jolt of thrust pushes him forward, toward her and the table that separates them. Then they are in the air.

"Tell me more about that day." A sadness shows on her. A caring.

"Alright. Like I said. I came home late. It was winter, got dark early. I pulled into the drive, her car was there. She was a nurse and it was her day off."

"What was her name?"

"My wife's?"

"Yes."

"Tabatha."

"Oh."

"So, I pull in next to her car and got out. Walked up to the door, let myself in. It was quiet. Again, not unusual. She might have gone for a run or was in the tub. Any number of things. Basically, I wasn't suspicious. I had no reason to be. Our marriage was good, happy. Anyway, I put my keys in the bowl by the door. Took off my coat and put it on the rack. Went into the kitchen. Got a glass of water and thought about going for a run, that I might even run into her on the trail beside our house. It was a pleasant thought. Then I heard something. Something upstairs that seemed off. A thud. Something landing hard. My first thought was that Tabby fell. Maybe getting out of the tub. I rushed up the stairs. I felt a tinge of fear, funny how you remember these things. Our bedroom door was ajar. Just slightly. I saw movement. Something go past the sliver of an opening. I rushed in. Pushed the door open. Then I saw it." Jack's words trail off as the pain twists his face.

"The vampire?" Abby's words are soft, barely heard.

A breaking in her voice. Jack can see the sadness overcome her expressions. He touches her hand, gently. Nods. Let's his own pain fade.

"Yes. It was Tristen. He had dropped her on the floor. The thud I had heard was her lifeless body as it hit the wood. The bastard just looked at me. Like I was interrupting something. Then I attacked. I didn't think. It was a mistake. Blind rage as the thought of my wife being murdered by this asshole in front of me sunk in. I wasn't any match for him. I was in good shape, but I worked in an office and there is only so much physical training you can do. Anyway, the thing grabbed me. Didn't say anything, just grinned this evil grin. Then the beating started. I was thrown against the walls, into furniture. My body was broken. I must have yelled out, because the neighbors showed up at the door of my bedroom. A couple of guys that Tabby and I had become close to. The vampire saw them. Dropped me and leap out the window into the backyard. I was told later that the police and an ambulance were called. That the vampire moved so fast that Charlie couldn't see it when he got to the window."

"And that is how you learned that monsters are real?"

"Yes. And how I began my hunt for Tristen. I woke up in the hospital. He had almost killed me. I had to go through physical therapy for months. Then the training.

Years of weight lifting. Martial arts. Weapons. Anything that could give me an edge. I read all the lore I could find and after two years I began small. I killed my first vampire. A fledgling. I needed information from it. I got what I needed and then left it for the sun. I watched it burn as the light came over the horizon. I learned what lore was true and what was not. No one trained me. I learned later that there were others like me. Then I learned that most were mad men seeking to torture and kill for sport. Serial killers that found a group that society didn't know or care about. So I stayed away, kept to myself. For the most part."

"It must have been lonely."

"It was. But I have a few people I trust, not many, but a few. Most of those I deal with, humans that is, are not the nicest people in the world. Arms dealers, pimps, drug dealers. They will get me what I want if I'm willing to pay. There's an underground for hunters like me. And I use them like all the rest."

"I see. And now we will end your hunt."

"I hope so. Tristen is hard to take down. He tends to disappear just as you get there. When we get to Miami I'll call a friend. See if she can help."

"I hope you find peace with this, Mr. Simpson. I hope that you can finally have the closure that you need. I know that after learning of the death of my parents, how that is, I was angry. I used knowledge to find a way to deal with my anger, my hate. You have found that being a hunter is what tempers your rage. A rage that you hold on too. I will do all I can to help you avenge your wife."

"Thank you." Jack's smile is bittersweet as he grasps

the cold cup of coffee in his hand. He realizes that he didn't see the stewardess place it on the table between Abby and himself. The memories, the pain, must have blinded him to all else in that moment of retelling the worst day of his life. He's only told one other person this tale. And he is going to need that persons help very soon. He looks up at the girl across from him. Her eyes closed. He is finding that she is someone he can trust, a jolt of fear as the thought sinks in. Then he lets it go and looks out of the porthole window at the clouds below them. Letting the serenity of the flight soothe him. His eyes close and he lets the tiredness take him.

Chapter 21
Gary

JACK'S BODY JUMPS AS A LIGHT TOUCH MOVES GENTLY across his arm. His eyes open to the familiar cabin of the private jet. The stewardess, at the bar, cleans the few items that he and Abby had consumed. His head turns to face the young woman that he is training. She smiles down at him in the slightly creepy way that only she can pull off. He rubs the little bit of sleep out of his eyes and stands. He can feel that the plane has stopped, that they have arrived.

"I must have drifted off." He fights the grogginess as he moves behind Abby as they walk toward the plane's exit.

"Yes. You snored a little, not to loud though. It was a pleasant flight. Janet, our stewardess, kept me company. She is a paid employee. Enjoys the life of flying around the world and found that the Society is a perfect way to do so."

"Ok. So, no supernatural stuff?"

"She's heard about it, but never seen anything. She

said she finds it hard to believe. It amazes me at times that the knowledge is not more freely known."

"That's what keeps those things alive. If everyone knew about them then they would be hunted down and exterminated. Like most predators that get in mankind's way."

"Yes, I assume you are correct there. It would make your job much easier if you had more support from the governments of the world."

"Our job, your in this too. Remember."

"Yes, it is taking some getting used too. And now that we are here in Miami, what's next?" He watches as the bags are pulled from the planes storage and dropped on a cart. The man is large. He looks over, an eye missing, grins and wheels the cart over to Jack and Abby.

"I think we should get to the hotel, it'll be dark in a couple hours and then I can call my contact." The large man waits with the three bags sitting on the cart, his smile grows. A few teeth are missing. Jack can see the excitement in his eyes.

"You're Jack." There is a smile in the words. The southern accent, New Orleans if Jack is placing it right. Jack looks the man over, taking him in. Ripples of muscle under the tight tee and baggy jeans.

"Yeah. And you are?" The caution taints the reply.

"This is Gary. He works on the planes. He's a mechanic, but helps with baggage sometimes." Abby nods at the large man. He smiles at her. Jack can see it's genuine.

"I want to wish you luck. Get that son of a bitch. I heard what you're here for. Everyone has. We know who you are. What you can do. If there is anything I can do to help, let me know. You're not the only one that piece of shit hurt." Jack watches as the smiling words turn to pain. The face twists as he hands the bags to the Jack and Abby. He turns.

"What happened?" Jack asks. The man's body stops. A shiver despite the humid heat of the Miami summer. "What did he do to you?"

"He killed my sister. Slaughtered her like a sheep. Drank her dry and left her body in her bed for us to find. I was the one that found her. I had to tell my mother. She was the best of us. And she was slaughtered by that thing. Make it hurt when you kill that monster. Make it suffer like my mother and father did when they put Maria in the ground. When they cried, holding each other. When my father took the shotgun and put it in his mouth and pulled the trigger. When my mother lost what little she had left and went into the hospital to never be right in the head again. Give that thing that kind of pain. Do that for all of us that have had to suffer that monster's slaughter." Jack watches the back of the man's head as he finishes. The sound of a sob coming from the large body.

"I will." Jack's words are soft, but heard.

There is anger in them that matches the mechanics. The large man walks away from the hunters. The sound of his grief heard over the incoming flights. Jack turns to Abby. Her eyes follow the man.

"I had no idea that had happened to him." The crack in her voice showing the empathy that is so uncommon from her.

"I understand it. I get it. Now we need to get to

work." Jack carries Abby's bag while rolling his own. She walks beside him, her second bag rolling behind her. "Where's the hotel?"

"By the ocean. It's an Art Deco building. The Society bought it in the twenties, the nineteen twenties. It helps fund our work and provides a place for any of our people that might need a place to stay." The pair of hunters move through the small terminal onto the sidewalk.

A black town car waits for them. The driver, a youthful man with chiseled features and a sparkle of a smile greats them with an open door. He swoops in, taking Abby's bag and putting it in the trunk with a grace that Jack wouldn't have expected from a man his size. He takes the bags from Jack and places them in the trunk with a gracious nod as he and Abby slip into the back of the car.

"Who's the pretty boy?" Jack grins as his counterpart's cheeks redden.

"Just a driver. Nothing more." Stumbling over her words. The grin on Jack's face grows. The driver slips into his seat, turns and smiles.

"Straight to the hotel or are there any stops you need to make?" The deep voice causes the pink to redden on Abby's flushed cheeks. Jack shakes his head slightly.

"No, I think the hotel will be fine. We'd like to settle in." The command is firm and the driver turns to face traffic, merging and speeding away toward the Miami beaches. Jack looks over at Abby, eyes on her lap. He touches her gently, she looks up. Embarrassment in her eyes.

"What is it?" His words light enough to be heard by her alone.

"I, was, well..." The words fumble out of her.

"You're embarrassed. Why?"

"He's cute and I, well..."

"You don't have to explain. And to be honest, the guy didn't notice. He's one of those good looking not so smart types if you ask me. So, let it go. Anyway, we have hunting to do and the last thing we need is our minds on anything other than that." His cocked brow clears the pink from her cheeks. A tight grin of agreement and she takes a deep breath.

"You are correct of course. We need to keep our minds on the task at hand." The stern confidence returns. Eyes front and determined.

Jack wonders if his resolve will be as strong in the next few hours. He hopes so. Then turns to watch the palm trees pass the window as the town car slips into the pink hotel drop off. Glass doors great them, framed by stucco the color of Abby's cheeks. He smiles and lets himself out of the car as the pretty driver pulls bags from the trunk and places them on a trolley.

Jack's eyes move over the entrance to the hotel. The sleek shapes that curve with neon lights. The glass doors open, a bell hop takes the trolley from the driver. Inside the shapes continue, chrome and glass chandeliers seemingly float above the guests as they are escorted to the chrome trimmed desk, its opaque glass top hiding the storage below. A man, tall and thin, his longish blonde hair swept back smiles a bright welcome at Abby as she steps before him. Jack watches. The guests. Young. Pretty. Wearing little more than swimsuits and drinking umbrella clad colors from punch bowl glasses. He looks back. Abby nods.

"Party town." She shrugs as she turns back to the lanky fellow punching in her information.

Keys slip across the glass. Abby slips them into a pocket, the bags are gone. Jack's eyes follow the youth moving in from the over filled pool. Abby moves beside Jack, looking up at him. Trying to read him.

"The room is ready?" His voice is soft.

Thoughtful. She nods. Walks to the elevator. He follows. Waits as the glowing button summons the way up. The giggling girls that are drunk is followed by the cat calls of the boys chasing them. The reflective doors open and Jack steps inside. Abby pushes the fourth four button and the pair are in silence.

"It seems that there is a faux spring break going on." Her eyes forward watch Jack through the smudged reflection. "The desk clerk apologized for the inconvenience."

"Their about your age, aren't they?" The door opens. A pair of swim trunk clad frat boys tumble into Jack. They bounce off of him.

"Sorry." The slur of alcohol slips from the talkers flushed face. "We're going down."

"This is our stop." The roll of Abby's eyes is lost on the pair of lobster shaded boys.

The door closes behind Jack and Abby as they step out into the hall. A bra hangs from one of the door handles. Beer cans litter the corners of the passageway.

"So much for high class." Jack shrugs as he follows Abby to their room. "Drunken college kids seem to be the norm."

"It's not. The hotel is normally, well, quite reserved. But it seems that we have arrived at one of those rare moments that Miami has become known for. This one is ours." The key card slips into the slot. Green light blinks positive and the door opens to the pastel colors of the beach.

"Our bags are here." Jack notices them tucked into the niche beside the bathroom. "And the beds look comfortable."

"Yes, it is normally a quiet place to stay. But, when the party goers arrive it tends to get out of hand. But we should be fine." Abby sits on the edge of the bed. Knees together, hands on them. The uncertainty in her eyes reminds Jack that she is still to new. That she still needs to know what comes next.

"I need to call my contact. Get together with her and find out if she knows anything about Tristen." Jack pulls his phone from his pocket.

His finger glides across the screen. The name looms. He touches it. The sound of ringing comes through the speaker. Abby's silence is a blessing. The ring ends.

"Jack? Jack Simpson? Is that you?" An attractive voice floats to his ears. Cheeks redden slightly as the memories rush into his mind. Abby's head cocks.

"Yes. It's me. I'm in Miami. We need to meet."

Chapter 22
Beth

JACK LOOKS AROUND THE LITTLE BAR ATTACHED TO THE restaurant. The wood beams, fake and easy to spot to a well trained eye, crisscross the ceiling giving a pattern of structure that is not there. The long wood table, running the length of the room has a few men in expensive suits and women in equally expensive outfits. Jack adjusts the tie that pushes the new fabric of the white shirt against his freshly shaved throat. The dim light is comforting to him as he scans the room for his contact. Abby, her pastel blue summer dress coming to mid thigh and exposing her pale shoulders, slips onto a bar stool. The bartender examines the fake I.D. His nod of approval is the only sign of acceptance as he takes her order. Jack slides in beside her, certain that Beth has not arrived.

"Sparkling water with lemon." Abby says politely. The bartender turns to Jack.

"What would you like, sir?" The bearded bartender

slides a bar napkin toward Jack. The boredom in the man's eyes. It's another comfort. He won't be interrupting.

"Whatever ale you have on tap. Doesn't matter which." The bartender's head nods slightly to the right, the beard moves up in the good answer response.

The slim man slips away from the hunters to retrieve the drinks. The other customers, waiting on tables or just wanting to get away from the college party that has taken over the beach community, sip their drinks in casual conversation.

"Your contact has not arrived?" It's more a statement than a question, but Jack nods regardless. "Have you know her long. Beth, that is her name?"

"Yeah. I meet her a couple years after I became a hunter. Baltimore. She was doing some training there. Learning some of the arts of her trade."

"Where you close?" A sparkling water with lemon is set in front of Abby, a beer in front of Jack. He takes the beer, sips it, sets it down.

"You could say that. She is the only woman I've slept with since the death of my wife." Abby watches him as the glass of amber liquid touches his lips.

"I see."

"She is something special. At least to me she is. Anyway, she can be a bit jealous and you don't want to get on her bad side. She's a great friend, but she can be difficult." Jack's eyes move across the bar, still no Beth.

"Why is she so dangerous. I thought she was an informant." The questions are not just in her words. Jack can see more behind those eyes. More she wants to ask. But she is refraining, holding back.

"You can ask me anything. We are partners, at least on this. You've earned my trust, even if it is clear you have a lot to learn. So. You want to know about Beth. First off. As I said we met in Baltimore. I was hunting a vampire there, a lead on Tristen. That's the recurring theme of it isn't it. Always Tristen. Anyway, I met her at her coven and she was assigned to help me. This vampire was causing some trouble for the witches there and I was already making a name for myself. So we got to work. Our working relationship moved to a more intimate relationship. I think, in my own way, that I loved her. Still do is some ways." Jack shrugs at his confession on love and continues. "So I found the vampire. Got what I needed, which wasn't much, and killed it. We parted ways not long after. Another lead took me away and she still had training to complete. Otherwise, I think she would have come with me. But that's not how it happened."

"There is something sad about all of it. You found another that you could care for and this Tristen took her away from you as well." Abby's eyes turned glassy with tears that refuse to fall. She dabs the wetness away.

"I never thought of it that way. But you're right. I could have been happy with her, Beth that is. But, her order and my revenge have kept us apart." He sips on the beer, the cold liquid reminding him of the winter he spent in Beth's arms. "And now I will see her again and, hopefully, I will avenge my wife and be able to move on. That is if he is still here."

"He is." The voice from the phone comes from behind the pair of hunters sipping their drinks.

Jack turns to see Beth. Her shapely form, curvy,

seductive. The red hair, long and braided. The dark green sun dress, tight. Freckled skin holds a wide grin showing the white teeth that sit behind the ruby red lips. Her green eyes, more emeralds that eyes, peer out at him with an affection he hasn't seen in a long time. He smiles. Stands. His arms wrap around her. Hold her tight. Let the smell of her natural perfume engulf his nostrils.

"It's been too long." The crack in his voice is slight, but both women notice.

"It has been." Beth's voice soft, caring. A love lost tainting the words.

"I'm glad you are here."

"The hunt continues I see."

"Yes." Jack says as Beth's green eyes move to Abby. Studying her. Taking in more than the physical features, moving into her soul.

"And this is?" The words are accusations. Tipped with venom.

"My assistant. I am teaching her a thing or two about the hunting world." Jack shrugs and lets the beer slide down his throat as the women take each other in.

"And why would you do that?" The jealous pain is there, Jack can hear it.

"Because her Aunt asked me to and she is the one paying for all of this." Jack is firm, unemotional. Beth nods, then slips into a seat beside him, opposite the girl he is training.

"Who is this Aunt? Anyone I would have heard of? Not many people are familiar with the things we are." More venom from the witch.

"Yeah, you know her. Carol Vinson. And before you

get worked up, that was a long time ago and she doesn't know that I am meeting you. I need your help, not the butcher of your clan." Jack positions himself between the women. Beth's eyes narrow. Hate fills the emeralds. Abby, turns to face Beth, remains reserved, quiet.

"You brought that cunt's little niece to me. I don't know if I should thank you for providing me a way to get back at that bitch or pissed that you are so fucking arrogant that you thought I could let that kind of history go." The bar has grown quiet as Beth's hate fills the room. Her shouts, match the anger of her body moving around Jack. Fists balled, eyes ablaze.

"ENOUGH." The growl stops the witch. She looks at him. Not understanding why he is stopping her. "This girl had nothing to do with that massacre and you know it. You would be killing an innocent and that, my dear, will get you banished from you order. Now, let's get one thing straight. Until I have Tristen's cold heart crushed under my heel, this girl is under my protection. Now get your head together and let's kill this fucker. Because, you know he has caused as much pain and suffering for your religion as he has me. I would assume that this girl's order has also suffered from that bastards hand. So, until it's over, we are allies. That or you can tell me what I need to know and walk away. Either way. I am killing that fucker." The growl, though softer, edges on murderous hate.

Beth nods, the rage subsiding, takes her seat. The room slowly returns to the conversations that Beth interrupted.

"We will have words after this is over, girl." Beth spits out as she drains the remains of Jack's beer.

"Enough, Beth. Now what do you have on Tristen?"

Beth's angry eyes soften as they move to face Jack. She sighs, letting the rest of her hate release her short frame.

"On Tristen himself, not much. You know the guy. Slippery. I'm sure that's why he's been around as long as he has. But I have something on one of his fledge's. He got picked up by a local hunter. Real scum bag. Works out of an abandoned garage. Uses the lifts to chain the magical's up and then tortures them. I don't think he does it for any other reason that it gets him off. Pretty much a serial killer that found a niche that will keep him out of prison." Beth waves down the bartender. "Red blend and another beer for my friend." Her smile calms the man's concerned brow and he rushes off to get the drinks.

"So, you have a location on this garage?" Jack leans against the bar, blocking Beth's view of Abby.

"Yeah. I can get you there tonight if you want. That vampire will be out until then anyway. Got another hour before the sun goes down and I could do with something to eat. And since that bitch of an aunt is paying, I could go for a steak." The hate glimmers in the witches eye as she sips the newly arrived glass of red wine.

Chapter 23
The Thin Man

THE SMELL OF THE SWAMP IRRITATES JACK AS BETH PULLS her Jeep into the parking lot of what was once a gas station. Off road sensations meet the trio as the Jeep traverses the mangled asphalt. Weeds brush against the metal doors with a scrap that does no damage. The Jeep stops, Beth pushes the shifter to park and looks over at Jack with a questioning eye.

"This is it. This is where the guy is. And the vampire that should know where Tristen is at. That is if this hunter hasn't killed the thing yet." Her voice is soft, secretive.

"Are you coming in with me or staying out here?" Jack asks as the door handle gives under his pull. A click and the swampy airs humid decay pulls a scowl out of him. "I hate the smell of the swamp. Damp and death."

The black leather work boot sinks into the broken grey asphalt. He pulls down the tee, a mummified monster with a tattered Union Jack and equally tattered red uniform lurches out at the viewer over the dead

Russian soldiers. Abby's light touch makes just enough sound to let herself be know. Beth, shaking her head, steps onto the decaying parking lot.

"Yeah, I'll come with you. You might need my help." Beth's tone is less than wanting, but her feet move her toward the filth slimed glass doors. Jack moves beside her, shrugs and bangs on the glass. Muffled movement from inside and the sound of angry words.

"Well, he's here." Jack shrugs again, then bangs louder on the glass. Bowing it in with each heavy slam of his fist.

"Go away." Hate filled yells come out of the door.

"Open up or I'll bust it down." Jack is loud, but the demand is calm and dangerous.

Silence. That is all they hear. Then the scruff of rubber on linoleum, mixed with dirt and paper. A scrap of metal on metal. Foot steps, soft. They stop short of the door. Just on the other side.

"Fuck you. Get lost or I'll bust you up." The threat is more whine than roar.

The pitch of the voice to high. Fear creeps out of the man inside. Jack can hear it. He can also hear where the whine comes from. Jack's boot slams hard into the door frame. The lock shears and the aluminum swings in. The crunch of a breaking nose. Scream of pain. Jack steps inside to see the garage hunter crumple to the ground, hands to his nose, blood flowing through the fingers, as tears burn past winced eyelids.

"Wrong answer." Jack kicks the steel pipe, streaked with rust away from the anorexic form in front of him. Short, dirty. The smell of unwashed humanity brings a sneer to Jack's already angry face. "You stink."

"It's my place. I can smell however the hell I want." The muffled words slip past the blood filled hands.

"I want to see this vampire you have in the back. The one you've been having so much fun with. I want to have a little chat and then I'll be on my way." Jack looks down at the skinny man, the rags of filth hanging loosely off of his body.

"And if I say no?" The sneer is an attempt to intimidate. Jack chuckles at the faux bravery.

"I'll slit your throat and let you bleed out on the floor. Then I will go have my chat with the vampire."

"Who the fuck do you think you are?" The bag of bones pulls himself off the floor, the sneer behind the remaining hand at his disjointed nose not hiding the look on his face.

"Jack Simpson." The words are calm. Quiet. The affect is something else.

Fear widens the thin man's eyes. The hand drops, the blood that has gushed over his lips, chin and shirt in full view. A stagger backward. He reaches for something to steady his wobbly legs, finds nothing, and stumbles back into the remains of a service counter.

"That can't be. You...you're a west coast hunter." The words, stuck in the thin man's throat, gurgle past the blood to get out. "You ain't suppose to be down here in Florida."

"Well, I am. And I don't plan to be here any longer than I have too. So, your guest please?"

"My what?" Question replaces the fear on the garage hunter's face.

"The vampire that I want to talk to. The one you

have strung up in the back. The one you've been cutting up for the past few days. That guest. I want to talk to that one." The patience in Jack's voice is all but gone. Beth and Abby can see the restraint in the man. The thin man shakes his head.

"Yeah, yeah, sure. This way. He's this way."

The thin man steadies himself on the edge of the counter, then uses the growing strength in his legs to shuffle toward a door that is slightly ajar. Jack motions for the women to stay and pulls a knife from his boot. The silver blade glistens in the sunset. A light flickers in the garage, the room the thin man has entered. Jack can see him, standing in front of the remains of a vampire. Jack watches the last shreds of light disappear behind the swamp and then the vampire's eyes open. They move slowly. There is pain there. Horrid pain. The marks on the creature. Silver cut, are deep in places. But not deep enough to kill. Only maim.

"This is him?" Jack steps into the smell. It is worse here than in the lobby. The work pit has filled with swamp water that has seeped up from the ground. Stagnant and revolting.

"It's him." The other hunter says calmly, his composure returning after the assault to both his body and mind.

"What did he tell you?" Jack moves closer. Looks at the fear in the vampire's dull eyes.

"Not much. Threats about his master at first. Then the fucker turned to begging. Then he got quiet. Just screams now. His face is pretty fucked up and I figure he is wanting to end it at this point. But not yet, eh you blood sucking fuck." The last is said with a gusto that make Jack cringe.

"I do the talking now. You step back and let me handle this."

Jack, the knife in hand, moves closer to the vampire. The creature's eyes move to the blade. More fear pulses through its near bloodless veins.

"What do you want?" The words are more rasp, though a touch of elegance remains.

Jack looks the vampire over. The shirt is gone, what remains has sunk to the bottom of the mire behind the vampire. In the swamp filled pit. Pants, slacks that must have cost plenty, are tattered. The scars all over the body. Most light, some deep. The face butchered by an accurate hand. Jack looks back at the thin man, a shameless grin on his face.

"You did this?" The disgust is heard in the vampire's ears, the other hunter only grins wider.

"Yeah." The pride turns Jack's stomach, the taste of beef and baked potato and bile mix as he swallows it back down.

"You want to die?" The whisper is low. Only the vampire's delicate ears can hear it. The vampire nods slightly. Just enough for Jack to see. "Then I will end this if you give me what I want."

"Deal" The raspy whisper is low and hopeful. "What do you want?"

"Your master. Tristen. Where is he?" Jack whispers. The vampire's eyes widen.

"I can't." The fear grows in the vampire. Jack looks on with hard eyes.

"You can. And you will. If not, I'll leave you with this mad man. He will keep you alive for years. Working slowly, painfully toward a death you will beg for over and over. I can end that. Just tell me where Tristen is." A tear fills the vampire's eye, then the other, then they begin to stream down the dirty pale cheeks, onto the floor. Muddy puddles begin to form below the raised feet of the vampire.

"You swear. You will finish me? I am ruined. Scarred so badly that I would have to ambush my prey. I couldn't seduce. The game. It is lost for me. The hunt is over. And only ten years of it. Only ten years." The tears flow. The vampire's body shudders at the painful movements of his weeping. Jack grips the knife, brings it to the vampire's neck.

"I swear."

"He is on the beach. A big house, lots of land. Beach front. There's a party tonight. A girl will be brought to him. He never goes out of the house on party nights. Sits in his study. Waits for the girl. Then he drinks her dry and listens to the youth frolic. That's what he calls it. Frolic. There'll be a lot of guards tonight. And he'll be protected. You should wait for another night." The words tumble over themselves. The vampire can't get them out fast enough.

The crying continues. The guilt of betraying his master and the hate he has for being left with the monster that disfigured him. He looks up at Jack as the blade slides through the thin skin of the vampire's throat. Blood, not much, but what little is left, pours onto the floor, giving it the closest thing to a cleaning in years.

"What the fuck man?" The thin man rushes at the hunter and the limp form that was an undead vampire only moments before. "I didn't say you could kill the fucker. I still wanted to have some fun with it."

"You'll thank me later." Jack wipes the blade on the lifeless bodies expensive slacks and returns it to his boot.

"The fuck I will." The anger is growing the thin man's voice.

"That vampire was turned by Tristen. Do you know who Tristen is?"

"What?" The thin man stumbles backward. "You're fucking with me?"

"No. That's why I wanted to talk to him. He told me where to find him, at least the last time he saw him. So, say thank you. Because if Tristen found out you had one of his, well let's just say that what you did to him would be child's play when Tristen got ahold of you."

"Oh, fuck. And you're going after Tristen. Isn't he like a couple hundred years old?" The thin man follows Jack through the lobby, out into the parking lot. Beth and Abby lean against the Jeep. They watch Jack as he moves toward them, motioning to get in the car.

"He's older than that. One of the oldest. And I'm going to kill him." Jack slips into the passenger seat. Beth, the engine running, backs onto the road and then drives away from the remains of the gas station. The thin man watching the Jeep grow smaller on the two lane back road.

Chapter 29
The Trio

"What is it?" Beth's voice is soft, caring as the Jeep pulls into the parking lot of the hotel.

Party goers, dressed in swimsuits and little else, make their way to the pool. Lights flash from the pool, the sound of club music invades the closed Jeep. Jack looks out at the group of coeds laughing, drinks in red cups.

"I don't want another one to die. All this killing. I have to stop it." His eyes remain focused of the mass of college aged men and women.

"You said the vampire told you there is a party tonight. At Tristens. That you should wait. Look, I know he said that a girl will be killed, drained. You have to step back. Getting yourself killed isn't going to help anyone. It's just going to get you killed." Beth's hand caresses Jack's thigh. He looks at her, determination in his eyes.

"Yeah. You're right. Tonight is not the night."

Jack pulls the handle on the car door. Steps into the music. Takes in the sea air. Helping to remove the tension that is building within him, the anger of feeling useless to prevent the monster that killed his wife from killing another tonight.

"Jack." The words are soft, but cut through the music and cheers of the crowd that is unseen beyond the high hedge that separates the pool from the parking lot.

"Yes, Abby?" His words are tired. He walks slowly, Beth on one side, Abby on the other. Guards against the foolishness they both know he is capable of.

"You will kill this vampire. We will help you. But not tonight. Tomorrow. We will plan tonight and kill tomorrow." There is a sympathy in her voice that surprises him. A caring that breaks from the business like manner.

He looks at her, the tension in the forced smile. The hope that he will not do what she is thinking he might. And he knows what that is. Go out. Find Tristen. Kill him.

"I'll wait." The reply, genuine, melts some of the tension from the young woman's face. He turns to Beth, she too smiles tensely. "Really, I will."

"Good, then we should get upstairs and figure out what we are going to do. Tristen isn't going to stick around long when he finds out you are in town. And he will. He has informants everywhere. The police, hotels, everywhere."

The pair moved through the crowded lobby. Mostly nude bodies moving past them. Happiness. Joy. Drunkenness. Things Jack has given up over the past ten years. Now, he is getting ready to end it and the feeling is bittersweet. He shakes this off as he and the women that are helping him slip past a group of frat boys into the elevator.

Abby pushes the floor and the elevator moves them up in silence. Jack's thoughts are on the mission. The way to get into that complex. He has nothing and knows it. The ding of the opening door brings him back to the here and now. The hall, empty and cleaned. The beer cans gone. The smell of alcohol remains. Loud moaning comes from a door. Abby reddens, Beth grins evilly. Jack ignores it. They enter the room. Quiet, except for the occasional thump of the base from the pool below. Jack moves to the window, looks down at the pool. The party is in full swing. Dancing, both in and out of the pool. The DJ, center stage and pumping up the crowds already high mood. Jack turns to the women with him.

"I'll order us something. Drinks and snacks?" Abby has the receiver of the hotel phone in hand.

"I could use some coffee and anything sweet. Chocolate if they have it. I think it's going to be a late night." Beth's eyebrow raises as she states what everyone is thinking.

"Yeah, coffee is good for me." Jack replies as he sits in the armchair beside the window.

"So what do you think, Jack?" Beth's tone is unemotional. Her eyes look at him, trying to read him. Abby hangs up the phone, sits beside the table as Beth slips, cat like, onto the bed.

"The food and coffee are coming." Abby's tone is neutral, returning to her normal self.

"This is what we need to do. Get the plans to this complex that Tristen has and find out where he sleeps. It's not going to be as easy as the last one. This vampire is old. Has a lot of tricks and is very careful. He is going to know that his daytime resting place needs to be hidden. So, any ideas of where this place is." Jack starts without much emotion. The mood is sullen in the room. All involved seem tired, strained.

"I think I have an idea. We can go by it in the morning. It'll be quiet then. Joggers mostly. It matches the little information we have. The deed, well that's more your thing Jack, but I can check around and see if anyone can get a real address. You should've called earlier, I could have had all this when you landed." Beth says, looking at the hunter slouched in the chair.

"Yeah, but we didn't have much notice, did we Abby."

"No. As for me, I can contact the Society and see if we have any updated information on Tristen and a hard address. Working it from both angles may provide a better result."

"The girl's right." Beth's words bring out a redness of anger in Abby's face.

"Well that's a start. When we get the information on where he is, we can figure out how to get in and where in the house he is at." Jack says quickly, trying to resolve the conflict between the women before it starts.

"It should be a day attack. Going in at night is just not smart. We'll have to figure out the guards, but I can use some charms on them to fuzzy up their minds." Beth grins.

"And I'll make sure we have the equipment we'll need. Scanners, weapons, and anything else. Get me a list and I'll make sure it is here." Abby replies.

The three hunters look at each other. No one has anything else to say. A buzz at the door and Abby moves to get it. A tired woman holds the handle of a cart. She smiles as she hands the snack plate and coffee to Abby, who slips her a tip. The door closes and the refreshments are placed on the table in silence.

"What now?" Abby asks, tiring of the quiet.

"We wait. Maybe coffee isn't such a good idea. Maybe we should get some sleep and get up in the morning. Scout it out. Do our research." Beth replies as she nibbles on a piece of cheese.

"Yeah." Jack says, disappointment in the words. He stands, moves to the door.

"Where are you going?" Beth asks, concern in the words.

"I need to clear my head. I'm going to go for a walk. I'll be back in a bit. Just need to work it out." He steps out into the empty hall. The sound of the music slightly louder. Beth and Abby watch as the door closes, worry wrinkling their brows.

Chapter 25
Jack

THE SMELL OF BEER AND CHEAP WINE HITS JACK AS HE exits the elevator. Swimsuit clad coeds cheer on a boy tipped upside down with a tap to his lips. The glazed look of drunkenness catches Jack's eyes. A flash of breasts and Jack gives them a forced smile. More cheers as the girl dances around topless.

Jack slips between young men and women, moving them when needed. Giggles float to his ears from the girls. The boys, either do not notice or glare and move on.

He steps through the back doors. The crowd, full of alcohol induced pleasure gives him no notice. He takes in the scene. The topless girls in and out of the pool. The boys attempting to woo them with drink and bravado. Some are going along, others have a look of disgust when the inevitable "let's go back to my room" is whispered into the opposing ear.

"Hey man, you're a little over dressed for the summer of love party." A deep male voice slurs out to Jack. He turns to see a monster of a kid. Ohio red, with matching hair, grinning at him. "Why don't you get into a suit and party hard with the rest of us?" The jolly red giant stumbles as a pair of girls grapple to keep him upright.

"Little old for this kind of party, but it does look like a good one." Jack's smile is slight. The boys eyebrows furrow. The pale skin reddens. Muscle tense.

"Really?" The growl is loud. Over the top. A step forward. The girls on each side failing to hold back the two hundred and fifty some pounds of muscle.

"Yeah, just going for a walk is all." Jack stands. Waiting. Watching.

"Well I think you're just a pussy that can't handle a good drink!" The arms pull away from the girls. The red hair moves forward on uneasy feet.

"Dude, he's old enough to be your dad." A tall pretty boy steps between the red headed giant and Jack. The giant stops, looks down, grins. Eyes focus on Jack. The heavy metal tee. The jeans. Work boots. And his age.

"Yeah, I guess he is." The giant shrugs and returns to the two girls waiting for him with another round of beers.

"Sorry about that." The pretty boy says with a smile as he moves closer to Jack. The blonde hair. Sparkle of a smile.

He'll make a hell of a politician. Jack thinks as the boy steps in front of him.

"Mongo tends to think that if you're not playing football or drinking you're wasting your time." The smile is infectious and Jack can't help but to chuckle.

"Yeah, well, he'll have to wake up when the college days are all over. Thank you for stepping in."

"Yeah, I'm kinda the dorm mom, if you know what I mean." The pretty boy nods at the crowd in red. Ohio State logos adorning the remain portions of the swimsuits and tees.

"So they sent you down to watch them?"

"Oh, no. I'm part of this madness. I'm the quarterback. We have training starting in a couple weeks and the last thing we need is for our starters to end up in jail for something stupid. Normally I wouldn't care. But, I have a chance to get into the NFL and I don't want one of these lugs to mess it up for me." The pretty boy shrugs.

"So you're protecting yourself?"

"And them. They *are* my teammates. Anyway, I had better get back to it."

"Have fun with that." Jack winks with sarcastic flair.

"Not likely." The grinning quarterback flashes back a winning smile as he wraps his arms round an equally pretty young man. Jack watches them chat as they watch the crowd, sipping beer from red cups and laughing at the antics that are in front of them.

Jack moves past the bodies of coeds into the parking lot. The sound of music from car radios blast a mash of unintelligible noise into the air. The smell of salt water, alcohol and human bodies mixes in an irritating odor. Here the coeds are clad in full swim suits and some are fully dressed. Locals have moved into the party scene, older and younger than the typical college student and Jack can see the slight tension that is building from the local boys being denied by the college girls.

He moves past this, letting the sidewalk take him where it will. The sound from the clubs creeps out of the buildings, as does the bright colored lights that paint the dance floors within. Groups of coeds mingle outside the clubs. Smoking, drinking, flirting. Jack moves past all this, his thoughts on the vampire that killed his wife. On the desire for revenge and the need to try to get past all that has happened to him in the ten some odd years since he learned of the existence of vampires and the other monsters that lurk in the shadows of society.

Jack stops. Listens. It is quiet, the sound of the waves lapping against the shore can be heard behind the beach houses that line the sidewalk that has lead him to this suburban silence.

Where the hell am I?

His eyes search for a sign. His wandering mind stops searching for landmarks. He glances at his watch. An hour has past. He knows the girls are worried. He knows that he needs to get back. A grim determination creeps across his face and he takes a step forward.

Need to find a place with a phone or a cab.

He strolls past the palm-tree lined street, taking in the beauty of it all. The full moon giving him some light in between the street lamps that hang above the roof tops.

This could have been mine. The house. The car. The wife. I had it, really did. Good career. My own little firm. A wife that loved me and I adored. A good life.

He stops. Looks at the wall. The sound of music coming from the other side. The party. The wall matches the description. It's only six feet tall. Nothing. He pulls himself up. Looks over at the crowded pool. The dark mansion beside it. The moonlight glimmer that ripples on the sea beyond the property. The dark suits. Sunglasses in the night. The pale skin, distinct even in the nights darkness.

Vampires. And their prey. This is the house he has been searching for, unconsciously. A man, human, with a dog walks the line of bushes that separate the crabgrass lawn from the wall that Jack peers over.

Jack drops to the sidewalk. Leans against the concrete blocks that separates Tristen from his knife. He feels for it. Caresses the hilt. A warm feeling of comfort grows inside him. The sound of the dog and owner moving past Jack's position as his ears strain for information. He waits. He hates this. The wait. A bark and a growl from the guard. The sound of them moving fast. Away from Jack. He peeks over. They have found a boy, a kid really, sneaking in. A grin forms on the hunters face as he kicks his legs over the wall and drops to the dirt below.

Bushes conceal him from prying eyes. The smell of the ocean brings fresh pain to his memories. Times with his wife. Times at the sea. Trips to Ocean Beach. Dinners in La Jolla. Clubbing in Pacific Beach. Bittersweet.

He moves. A sprint across the grass.

Just like the last time.

The thought brings a smile to his lips as he wills himself to believe the outcome will be the same. But it is dark. The vampire is not in his tomb. This one is old. Dangerous. He could kill Jack with little more than a flick of his finger, the power the monster holds. But it is too late and Jack knows it. It has begun.

Jack creeps along the wall. A color that he can not fathom in the shadows that consume his form. He freezes. The sound of movement. A man in a suit. A man, not a vampire. He strolls along the bush lined concrete block wall. A cigarette hanging loosely from his lips. The cherry brightens as smoke is pulled into his lungs. The black skin clearly visible from the cigarettes light. A cloud of smoke trails past the man as it exits his nose. The stroller moves past Jack and around a corner. A quick look and Jack confirms he is alone. A window is above him.

He peers in. Books line the walls. A small wooden desk and leather chair sit at one end of the room. A pair of leather chairs and an end table that is between them holds a light that would bring illumination to the room if it was on. The two chairs, high backed and facing into the room, can only be seen from their backs. A slight crack in the window. Jack tests it. It moves up silently and smoothly. He pushes it up, slips into the room. Stands, letting his eyes adjust to the darkness.

"Hello, Mr. Simpson." The voice brings a chill to Jack's spine. A slightly high voice. An accent that is a mix of many. The voice of Tristen.

Chapter 26
Tristen

JACK FREEZES AS THE SOUND OF THE VAMPIRE'S WHISPER reaches his ears. His eyes flicker across the room, searching for the source of the sound. He is blinded. Eyes squint as the light burns into his eyes. He blinks away the discomfort and focuses on the vampire in front of him, slowly pulling itself from an armchair. The tall lank figure looks at Jack, the smirk sickening Jack as it moves around the chair toward the hunter. The creature's suit is black, fashionable. A pale yellow shirt under it with a black tie. Jack's eyes wander over the vampire. Taking in the pale skin, the black hair, long and pulled back into a ponytail. The smile, fangs glimmering between the sliver of lips, has a dark look to it.

"So you are the hunter Jack Simpson, yes?" The words are smooth, velvety.

"Yes." Jack braces, waiting for the attack.

"And I killed your woman. Years ago. In San Diego."

"Yes."

"Ah, your woman. I remember her, if that can be believed. It was the taste of her blood, rare. You see, vampires enjoy the flavor of blood like you humans savor a good wine. It was AB negative. A rarity and such a vintage. So little of the fats and chemicals that are so common in this day and age. She ate well and exercised I assume."

"Yes." Jack's words hiss out of him as his eyes drill into the vampire standing across from him. A white hand moving slowly, in a caress, across the leather chairs back.

"You see, it was that blood. The rarity. It was intoxicating. I had to have it. And the taste was worth the wait. I stalked her from the store the night before, I doubt you knew that. You were home that night and I had no desire to kill two humans for the flavor of one. I'm not sure why, it would have saved me the trouble of getting you here." The grin on the monster across from Jack brings his blood to a boil.

"Getting me here?"

"Oh, did you think things hadn't been arranged? But I'll explain that later. First, your deceased wife and the taste of the blood that flowed out of her and onto my tongue. I have to admit, you have excellent taste, though I doubt it was the taste of such a rare vintage that attracted you to her."

"No, it wasn't." Jack growls.

"I bet it was the ass. Very shapely. Indulgent if I may say so. I assume you two had very passionate nights before I found her. Before, well I must say, had my little drink." The wink of the vampire's eye brings a scowl to the hunter's lips. He holds, restraining for the right moment.

"Yes, she was a true beauty. A shame to waste in a way, but I could not help myself. As I'm sure you could not when you first took her. Certainly not her first. There had to be others before you. Possibly during your time together. Oh, a lovely creature like that must have drawn the attention of many suitors, even if she was currently taken. Is that not how the world has become. Yes? So similar to when I was made." The playful smile that dances across the fanged lips taunts Jack. His hand grips tight, balled into white fists of anger.

"No, there was no cheating." Jack's voice is hardly heard, even to the vampire's delicate ears.

"So certain of that. How naive. Though, you may be right. I did not stalk her long, just long enough to find you not there. That is when you came in. Found us in our embrace. She was drained of that delicious blood at that point. Dead. And now you are here."

"Yes, I am here."

"To exact revenge. To kill me, correct?"

"That's the plan."

"And you decided the best time was at night, when I would be roaming my complex. How amusing."

Tristen watches Jack fumble with the question. Lets the foolishness sink in. Watches the hunter's discomfort grow.

"You see, that boy, the one you put out of his misery. Well he was one of mine. A foolish lad, not as foolish as you, but foolish none the less. He upset me, the reason is not important, so I had him taken by that hunter. I believe you meet him. That was arranged. Do you think your little band of scholars and witches are the only ones with resources and spies. Oh, no, Mr. Simpson. I have my one little band of rogues that have infiltrated all of the organizations that might seek to destroy me."

"And the boy, the one that was sacrificed to get you here. I can sense that it bothers you, even if he was a vampire. So I will explain to you the reason I sacrificed his life to get you before me. You could almost say you were summoned in a way. It was a girl. One that had a rare blood type, not as rare as your wife's, but rare it was. She was to be mine and mine alone. This youth took her. Only a little taste. Small and not fatal. But enough to annoy me. Others knew of what he did and it could not be allowed. So I sent him on an errand. Had my spies inform the hunter of his exposed state. Then he was in that monster's hands. And I can see by your look that you find that ironic, me calling that hunter a monster when you stand before an ancient one. But his methods are such that he has become one. Unlike you my talented killer."

"But you see, I am not one without a sense of justice. Right now, he is dying. Tortured as he did to those of my kind. Slices ever so slightly. The pain, I would assume, is intense. Humans are working the job, with the promise of being turned. Which may or may not happen. I only keep promises that work to my favor."

"As for you're little band in that pink monstrosity of a hotel. They to will be taken care of soon enough as well. In due time. I want them to learn of your death and feel that pain sick into them. Let it linger of weeks. Then I will have them exterminated like the vermin they truly are. But for now it is you and I, Mr. Simpson, or may I call you Jack?"

"You can call me anything you want." Jack's eyes dart around the room, desperate for anything he can use as a weapon. A slight comfort comes to him as the hilt of the dagger touches his leg.

"There is nothing here that you can use to kill me with. I am quite safe." The grin is light, humorous in its feel. It turns dark, as does the look the vampire gives the hunter that stands open to attack. "Unlike you, Jack."

The vampire has Jack by the shirt before he can register his movement. Jack's feet leave the hardwood floor. His body moves through the air as arms, not looking strong enough to preform, launch his body toward a bookcase attached to the wall. Jack's shoulder screams out in pain as it connects with the cherry shelf. His body drops to the floor with a thud. Eyes water. The grimace of pain pulses through him. He looks up to see the vampire grinning at the crumpled hunter.

"You see, I am much older than any of you think. Even other vampires have no idea of how old I am. I watched Rome start as a little hamlet of thugs on a hill. I watched it grow. Become a power like few have ever seen. I stayed in the shadows, my condition preventing me from any glory. But my whispers, the senators all but welcomed my advice."

The vampire lifts Jack, one handed, looks him in the eyes. The hunter winces at the pain.

"I watched the world descend into chaos and feudalism. A time that I found quite convenient to me and my kind. Watched humanity return to it's animal base in a Europe that I loved. Watched the empire I so loved fall into the hands of fools and madmen. But I drank with an ease that I have not had since."

"Watched the age of intelligence return. The Age of Enlightenment. Of free men. And vomited at the thought of it. The disgust. Men free to do as they wish. Not all men. And that was one of the things I loved of this age. The hypocrisy of it all. Men free. Unless your skin was too dark. Your eyes too almond shaped. No, it was an age of Europe and nothing more. Enslaving the rest of the world. And that I gloried in. And the women. Nothing more that possessions to the men that owned them. Did you know, Jack, that a woman could not own property? That is was illegal throughout the White world. Oh, yes. And their bodies. Mere toys for the men that owned them."

"Yes. I did." Jack growls as he leans back on the books and waits for an opening to attack.

"But enough of my commentary of the way things were." The glare from Tristen is repulsive and frightening.

The vampire moves across the room with a speed that is barely comprehended in the hunter's mind. Strong white hands pull him off the books, bring him off his feet. Then a flick of the vampire's wrist and Jack's body soars across the room. He back smashes into the wall and crumples under his weight. He drops to the floor, uses the good arm to pull himself up. Glares at the vampire that struts slowly toward him. Then he moves. Fast. Unexpected. He slams into the middle of the vampire, his waist meets Jack's shoulder.

Tristen grabs, pulls the hunter from under him, whips

him in front of him. Lears into the hunter's eyes as Jack glares back, his eyes filled with hate.

"Clever. But useless. You can not defeat me, boy. I am immortal. I am a vampire. I can not be killed. Not by you. Not by that whore in her big house in New York. Not by that little slut from Germany that likes to think she runs San Diego. No, Mr. Simpson, I can not be killed."

Jack's leg moves fast. He knows his time is done. Tristen is finished torturing him. It is now or he is going to be dead. His knee moves fast and hard into the vampire's groin. The grip loosens. Jack slips out from the pale hand holding him. The vampire glares as it straightens. It lunges, fast. Merely a streak in the man's eyes. But there is enough time for him to move. Hands slamming into the over-extended vampire. A push, the ability to re-adjust lost. The table collapses under the vampire's weight. Tristen's body grows limp. Jack stands over him. Looks down at the monster, a table leg sticking out of his heart. The fixed glare on the monster's face. Jack returns the glare, his hate growing.

"You smug fuck. You thought you couldn't be killed. Well, I'm going to kill you for what you did to my wife. And for the threat to my friends. And for all the others that you have killed over the centuries. Tonight I end you."

Jack's hand slips to his boot. The dagger glints in the light. He places it on the vampire's throat. Watches the eyes as the silver blade slices through the ancient flesh. The head rolling away from the body. Blood covers the floor.

Jack stands. He walks to the bookcase, pulls the books off of the shelves. Moves to the crushed table. Takes the lighter that lays beside the candle. Returns to the books. Lights one. Lets the flames grow. Tosses it in a corner. Repeats with other books. The blaze grows. Smoke bellows out of the open window. Jack follows, his feet landing on the soft grass.

The sound of the party is uninterrupted. No guard in sight. He rushes to the wall. Leans against it. Sinks down. Lets the thought of his revenge, finally achieved, sink into his soul. A grin creeps across his lips.

"I did it honey. I killed the bastard." His whisper is soft, loving as his mind drifts. Fatigue taking him. Fatigue that has been building since his wife died. His eyes close as the flames grow across from him. Bushes hide him from the frantic guards and guests that scream in terror as the house turns to inferno. As his body surrenders to sleep, his mind tries to make him move, but it is useless. His thoughts drift off as darkness encompasses him.

Chapter 27
Carol

THE SMELL OF DISINFECTANT AND STARCH DRIFTS LIGHTLY into his nostrils. His closed eyes take in the smell, wondering if this is the smell of the afterlife.

Cleanliness is close to Godliness. The thought drifts through his mind.

His last thought, of stumbling into the brush outside of the burning house that belonged to his nemesis. To Tristen. A smile creeps across his face, the thought of the vampire dead. Gone forever. This makes whatever he has gone through, whatever he will face, worth it. A new smell arrives as the sound of a heavy door softly opens and closes. Rose lotion. The smell of his grandmother. Fond memories flirt with his mind. Broken by the tap of a thick heal on a hard floor.

"Mr. Simpson?" The voice is soft, caring in it's gravelly way. "I have come to confirm that you have killed the vampire Tristen and in doing so have rid the world of a monster unlike anything we have seen in the past."

Jack's eyes open to the wrinkled smile of Abby's aunt. Her spotted hand, thick with lines, touches his gently. She sits beside him, the chair higher than it should be as he shifts to look at her with groggy eyes.

"So he is dead?" The words are clear, though the thoughts are only coming into focus.

"Yes. We have a member on the police force. He was there. Confirmed the remains belonged to the vampire. The ash was tested and proved positive. No one else was injured in the blaze. It has been ruled an accident. A candle, left unattended, set the library ablaze and the flames moved through the house. Again, Tristen was the only victim."

"Good. But, where am I?" Jack looks around the stark hospital room.

"In a private hospital room. You are still in Miami. It is the second day since the death of Tristen. Your wounds are on the mend, surprisingly quick. I believe that the doctor is planning on releasing you soon.

"And how did I get here? I collapsed in Tristen's complex. Passed out."

"Yes, that. It seems that when you did not return to the hotel, my niece and your former lover took it upon themselves to find you. Beth knew the location of Tristen's lair. At least she believed she did. Some kind of connection she has with you. They arrived to the fire engulfing the home. Your witch used her talents to locate you and get you to the other side of the wall. Levitation is a very useful talent. They brought you here, and it was kept quiet from the authorities."

"Oh."

"And that brings the next issue."

"And what might that be?" His eyes look into hers.

"You, Mr. Simpson, the issue is you." The smile grows, widens in a grandmotherly way. Jack is disarmed by the look. Kind, soft. So unlike the woman he spoke to before.

"What of me? My goal is done. Tristen is dead." His shrug is defeat.

"Yes. But what will you do now?" The softness of the words have tension, something he hardly noticed before. He looks at her, seeing the fear in her eyes.

"I haven't really thought about it. Go back to architecture. My license is still good." Even as he says it, he finds the thought of sitting at a computer, day in and day out, gives a bitter taste to life.

"You could come work for us." There is hope in her eyes. Almost a begging of a sort. He looks at her. Curious. Unsure.

"And be a slave for whatever you feel is the right amount of time?" No malice in the question as he looks at her, he is wanting an answer.

"No. You have proven that that is not needed. I think you would be a full member, with all rights and privileges. You would continue to train my niece. She would be your apprentice and she would help you navigate our rules. If that is acceptable."

"Yes, yes I think it would be. I would like a free hand in my hunting though. To choose my prey. To seek out those that are the most dangerous."

"Of course. I believe that would be beneficial for both of us. And my niece would receive a first rate education."

The uncertainty disappears, as a smile of true happiness appears on the winkled lips.

"And where is she?" Jack's eyes dart around the room, the smile remains.

"She is in the hall, waiting. Her and your friend. Beth, I believe is her name. We had words earlier. A discussion really. On the subject of The Society and her order. It was decided that we should consider working together, that it would be in both our interests to do so. I have a meeting with her superiors tomorrow."

"That sounds easy."

"Hardly. I may have said we had words. There was some hysterics coming from your former lover. Yes, she told me. After our spat. But it has been resolved, at least the resolution has begun."

"Good. They're good people."

"So I have learned over the past few years. But I keep you from those that have more affection for you than I do. And, Mr. Simpson, I do feel a certain affection for you. Not for what you have done for my niece. Not for destroying one of the most dangerous vampires on the planet. Not for helping with the other problem in upstate New York. No, it is for your ability and kindness that you have shown to my niece. She is really quite fond of you. The father that she never had. Oh, some of the tutors have been fatherly. But you have shown true caring for the girl. And that alone places you among those beloved to me."

Jack watches the old body move slowly off of the raised chair. Her cane held firmly in her hand. She opens the door with a strength that Jack wouldn't have guessed at. She turns and winks. A childish glitter in her eye, then she disappears into the hall.

Jack's smile overflows as Beth and Abby rush at him. He knows that he is where he belongs. That he has what he lost so long ago. A family.

Printed in the United States
by Baker & Taylor Publisher Services